JESSICA BECK

THE DONUT MYSTERIES, BOOK 25

DEVIL'S FOOD DEFENSE

The First Time Ever Published!

The 25th Donut Mystery.

Jessica Beck is the *New York Times* Bestselling Author of the
Donut Mysteries, the Classic Diner Mysteries, the Ghost
Cat Cozy Mysteries, and the Cast Iron Cooking Mysteries.

To my dearly beloved,
For never giving up on me!

When kindly old Gray Vincent is stabbed after Movie Night in the Park, everyone is puzzled as to why anyone would want to kill him, but when Gray's past sins are revealed, it's just amazing to the folks in April Springs that the man was able to keep his secrets so long, and so well. Or did he? Was Gray struck down because of his past, or because of something that happened more recently? With Jake away on family business, Suzanne and Grace are determined to find out as they dig into the past and try to discover who killed him, and why.

CHAPTER 1

MOVIE NIGHT IN THE PARK was an annual celebration in my hometown of April Springs, North Carolina, held to honor the arrival of spring as well as the naming of our town. It was usually a time of fun and food, a chance to embrace the official end of winter and prepare for the eventual coming of warmer days, though we often had to bundle up for the outdoor movie showing.

Dial M for Murder had been available as a free rental this year, and Momma, head of the committee, had taken advantage of the opportunity to save the town budget a little money. Besides, it was an old favorite of my mother's, and I wouldn't put it past her to force her taste onto the rest of the town in such an overt manner.

Unfortunately, murder was exactly what we got, and not just on the big screen.

Homicide had found its way back to April Springs, and once again, I was right in the thick of it.

CHAPTER 2

"**I** CAN'T BELIEVE WE'RE BACK AT the shop again already," Emma said with a sigh as she started her dishwashing routine for the second time that day. We'd finished our normal run and had closed up Donut Hearts at eleven that morning, which was our regular schedule, but our break this time had been a short one, since we'd both come back to the shop three hours later to start it all again.

"Remember, it's for a good cause," I said. I was glad that I'd taken a nap during our time off. I knew that I'd need all of the rest I could get, and it hadn't been too tough to find the time, given the fact that Jake was in Raleigh visiting his older sister and her children. Sarah had been raising Paul and Amy alone for most of their lives, and my husband made pilgrimages there every so often to give them a man's influence in their lives. The kids loved him, and his older sister absolutely adored him. She'd been a big fan of Jake's first wife too, and I constantly had the feeling that she would never think that I'd be good enough for her little brother. I did my best to accompany Jake to Raleigh every now and then, but I would have been lying if I said I wasn't happy to have the movie night festivities as an excuse to miss this particular trip.

"Are we at least making a little money ourselves for the event?" Emma asked. Since she'd taken over the donut shop two days a week on a regular basis, she'd become much more interested in the financial aspects of running Donut Hearts. I wouldn't say that we had a competition going about who made the shop the most money during our respective times at the helm, but it was a friendly rivalry that did nothing but help our bottom line.

"Yes, I won't make the mistake of ever just giving them away again." I'd made that error once in the past, and the cost of the supplies we'd provided had nearly wiped out two months' worth of profit. I was all for contributing my services to a worthy cause, but I wasn't going to give up my supply costs, too, and if we could make a little something for our trouble over and above that, I thought it only fair. "Our donuts, coffee, and hot chocolate will all be on sale at their regular prices, but we're donating half the profits this evening to the Food Bank." The bank was a relatively new group in town, and they provided meals for those who couldn't afford them. It had helped me as well, since our overages went straight to them every day. I hated throwing out good donuts just because no one had chosen them that day, plus, it gave me a tax write-off, something that was dear to my heart, especially as April 15th approached.

"I'm glad the shop is getting something out of it, too," Emma said.

"Do you mean besides that warm and fuzzy feeling we'll get from helping out a good cause? Our expenses will be taken care of, and there will be a little extra as well. Don't worry," I said with a smile as I finished icing the cake donuts we'd be offering for sale that evening. We were making a less varied batch of donuts this afternoon, mostly just sticking with our bestsellers. "Are you ready to make a giant batch of your hot chocolate? It's going to be chilly tonight."

"I'll be ready," Emma said. She was usually in charge of the drinks at Donut Hearts, offering special blends of coffees, and on occasion, our famous hot cocoa.

I nodded as I started mixing the yeast donut recipe I used in our large floor mixer. The motor was loud enough to discourage conversation, but that was fine. Our break would be soon, and we'd have plenty of time to chat, with the added benefit of having daylight at our disposal instead of sitting out front in the dark. Once I had everything in the recipe nicely incorporated, I pulled out the dough paddle and covered the mixer's massive bowl with cling wrap. Emma was already standing by the kitchen door waiting for me.

"Would you mind trying something for me before we take our break?" she asked me as we walked out into the dining and display area of the shop. There was a small urn set up out there that hadn't been there when we'd come into the shop earlier.

"What have you been up to?" I asked. I noticed that she'd snuck up front a few times as I'd been working, but I knew better than to ask what she'd been doing.

"I'm trying a new hot cocoa blend," she said.

I tried not to hide my surprise. After all, Donut Hearts might be known for the fried rounds we offered to the public, but our hot chocolate had a loyal following of its own, and I was no more eager to mess with the recipe than I would be to take lemon-filled donuts off the menu. "Are you thinking this will take the place of our regular recipe?"

"What? No! Of course not. We'd have a riot on our hands if we tried something as silly as that."

I thought she might be overexaggerating, but I agreed with her assessment that folks would be displeased. "So, this is meant to be 'served with' instead of 'replacing'," I said to clarify.

"Absolutely. I'm not sure if I like it, though. I've been playing with recipes so much lately that I've lost my taste for hot chocolate altogether. Does that ever happen to you with donuts?"

I grinned and patted both hips. "Take one guess and tell me what you think."

"You're lucky," she said.

"Yes, that's exactly what I call it," I said, laughing as I

accepted the cup she offered me. I took a sip, trying to keep my expression neutral as my senses were overwhelmed with flavored extract.

"Well, what do you think?"

"It's certainly minty, isn't it?" I asked, forcing myself to take another sip once the shock to my taste buds died down a little. Honestly, it tasted as though she'd added more mint flavoring than cocoa powder.

"It's too strong, isn't it?" she asked, clearly worried about my lack of immediate endorsement. "I was afraid of that."

"Why don't you try halving the mint extract next time," I suggested. "Or maybe cutting it to a third of what you used this time."

"It's really hard getting flavor proportions right, isn't it?"

"Don't get discouraged," I said as I patted her shoulder. "You've seen how many donuts I try that never make it to the menu. You're on the right track, so don't give up when you're so close."

"Thanks," she said, clearly grateful for the words of encouragement. Why wouldn't I? What I'd told her had been true. I threw away far more new experiments than I ever added into the donut flavor rotation, and some of them still held memories of good ideas gone horribly, indelibly wrong.

"Remember that mint julep donut I tried last year for the Kentucky Derby? I get queasy just thinking about it, and it's been nearly a year since I took a bite."

"All I remember is that I thought you were exaggerating, so naturally, I had to take a bite to see for myself," she said with a smile.

"You didn't make that mistake again, did you?" I asked her, laughing.

"No, but who's to say I won't make it again?" she asked happily. "Would you like some regular coffee for our break?"

"No, I might just grab a bottled water," I said.

"To help you get the taste of my hot cocoa out of your mouth?" she asked, laughing to show that she was only kidding.

"Actually, I'm trying to hydrate for this evening. You don't have to work the shop with me, you know. Won't your young man be disappointed?"

"We broke up yesterday. I swear, I'm having the hardest time finding a good guy. Where are they all hiding?"

"Don't ask me. It took me forever to find Jake. All I can say is don't give up yet."

"I'm not about to. Anyway, I'd be happy to work the shop for the movie. You know what we should do?"

"What?" I asked. Emma needed a win after her hot cocoa disaster, and if I could make it happen, I'd do it. She wasn't just an employee; she was also one of my best friends.

"We should go get our donut cart that we use for street fairs and station it out in the park."

We had a pushcart that we used for sales away from the shop, but it wouldn't hold a tenth of the cake donuts I'd already made, not to mention the yeast ones that were still to come. "Do you think there's enough space on it?"

"Not 'instead of,'" she said with a grin, "'along with,'"

"I like it," I said. "I'll take the cart, and you can stay in here where it's warm."

"We'll alternate," she suggested. "That way neither one of us has to stay on their feet the entire time."

"I like it," I said. "The cart's over at my rental building. Do you mind walking over there with me on our break to get it?" The building had been a last and surprising gift from my father, and so far, it had brought me nothing but bad luck. The attorney who'd first rented from me had been murdered inside, and understandably enough, I'd had a tough time getting anyone to lease it since.

"Sounds like fun," she said. "Honestly, I wouldn't mind stretching my legs."

"Then let's go get it," I said.

It was a beautiful afternoon, crisp and clear, and at least for the moment, the pollen count was below normal, probably due to the heavy rains we'd been having lately. I knew the nursery rhyme mentioned April showers, but March had given us quite a few deluges already. As we walked past ReNEWed, Gabby Williams's gently used clothing store, I glanced in through the window to see what was new. Gabby had positioned a mannequin in the window dressed for a formal evening in a shimmering green dress that probably cost more used than my entire wardrobe I normally wore in a week. After that, we passed Patty Cakes—the bakery building—and Burt Gentry's hardware store, and then we turned off Springs Drive onto Viewmont Avenue—between the city hall and the town clock—past the police station, and then to my lonely little empty office building.

"Let me get my key," I said as I found the correct one and unlocked the back door of the place. The cart was sitting by the door, so it was simple maneuvering it out. I was glad that it was so easy to push down the sidewalk back toward Donut Hearts. I was definitely running out of steam.

As we approached city hall on our return trip, I spotted Gray Vincent hurrying past. Gray was a good customer at the donut shop, but I hadn't seen him around in the past few days. The man had to be in his seventies; more than a little bit portly, he sported a white beard and a thinning scalp, as well as a faded scar along one cheek. When I'd asked him about it, he said that he'd been kicked in the face once by a mule. I wasn't sure if that was true, but it was clear he didn't want to talk about it, so I'd dropped it. Our mayor, George Morris, had tried to get him to play Santa for the last Christmas parade, but Gray had predictably declined. He was a bit of a hermit, living in a cabin outside of town that to my knowledge no one ever visited. In the twenty years I'd known him, I hadn't seen him out on a single date, or even have any legitimate good friends. Gray clearly liked to be by himself, plain and simple. I found him nice enough, though. He usually had a smile and a nod for me whenever he came into Donut Hearts. "Gray. Hey, Gray! Hang on a second."

To my surprise, he sped up at the sound of his name being called, and before I could catch up with him, he'd vanished into city hall.

"That's odd," I told Emma as I turned to face her. As I did, I spotted someone ducking behind the building. Was someone actually following us? Or perhaps they'd been trailing Gray. Then again, it could just as easily have been my imagination.

"What is?" she asked. "Did you really expect Graybeard to stop and chat with you in the middle of town?"

"His name's Gray, Emma, just Gray," I corrected her.

"Sorry. Most folks in town call him that. I didn't mean any disrespect by it."

"It's fine," I answered, aware that I was being a little terse with her. I had a soft spot in my heart for the man. After all, who among us didn't feel like being a recluse at some point in our lives? "You know, he told me once why his name was Gray."

"I always just assumed it was a nickname," Emma said as we pushed the cart past ReNEWed and to the front of Donut Hearts.

"No, it's his actual legal name. Evidently his parents wanted to name him Gary, but the nurse misunderstood and wrote Gray on his birth certificate instead. They could have had it changed, but it would have cost five dollars to resubmit the form, and he said that his folks were notoriously cheap. By the time he could do it himself at eighteen, he'd decided that he liked that it was different."

"Did he actually tell you that story himself?" Emma asked me with amazement.

"Yes. Why?"

"I just didn't know that he could talk that long at one time," she answered with a grin.

"I'll admit that he's gotten worse over the years. I heard the story when I first opened Donut Hearts. He wasn't nearly as much of a hermit in those days. He pretty much stays to himself on his land now."

"You don't have to tell me. There are so many warnings and No Trespassing signs posted there, I doubt anyone has gotten past his perimeter defenses in years. His mailbox is at the head of the drive into his place, and just after that, there's a gate that's always locked, and a bend in the path that shows nothing of what's beyond it."

"How do you know so much about that?"

"When Mom was teaching me to drive, we drove down that way and used it as a turnaround. There's never any traffic out that way, so it was perfect for practice. He's even got security cameras posted at the gate, if you can believe that."

"The man clearly likes his privacy."

"I guess so, but does he have to lock himself away from the world?" she asked.

"We don't know much about him. He could have had a hard life before he came to April Springs," I said as we went back inside. The cart would be fine right where it was out in front of Donut Hearts. Not only could we keep an eye on it as we worked, but nobody was going to steal it in broad daylight.

As I got to work on the next stage of the yeast donuts, Emma asked me, "I just kind of assumed that he'd always lived in April Springs."

"He has for as long as you've been alive," I said with a laugh. "One day he just showed up after buying the old Parsons cabin. The gate went up before he moved in, but he said at the time that it was because he was at the end of nowhere, and he wanted to keep it safe and secure."

"Well, he's managed to do that," she said. In an abrupt change of subject, Emma asked, "How long is Jake going to be in Raleigh?"

"I'm not sure," I answered.

"Are you two having problems?" Emma asked me, clearly concerned about his absence.

"No, of course not. Why do you ask?"

"I'm just kind of surprised you didn't go with him. You know Mom and I would have been happy to run the shop for you if you needed to be there."

"I know, and I appreciate it, but I didn't want to let Momma down. This film night is her baby, and I wanted to be here in case she needed me."

Emma frowned. "And that's the only reason you stayed in town?"

She wasn't going to let me slide on it; I could see that clearly enough. "It's the main one, but the truth of the matter is that his sister, Sarah, doesn't like me," I blurted out.

"You? Who doesn't like you? I'm having a hard time believing that. You're extremely likeable, Suzanne," Emma said, puzzled.

"I know, right?" I asked her with a grin, feeling better after saying it aloud.

"Did you do something to her, maybe even something you weren't aware of doing? If you did, maybe an apology would smooth things over between you."

"What I did, I refuse to apologize for," I said firmly.

"Wow, that must have been a real doozy. Don't keep me in suspense. What did you do?"

"I had the audacity to marry her brother," I said. "She was a big fan of Jake's first wife, and she told me in no uncertain terms when we first met that nobody would be good enough for him in her eyes, no matter how happy I made him."

"Give her some time. I'm sure she'll come around eventually," Emma answered.

"Maybe, but I didn't have the strength to deal with her this weekend," I replied. "Movie Night gave me a perfect excuse to beg off from going on the trip."

"Well, I for one am glad that you're here. We're going to have fun." She paused and then smiled for a moment before speaking. "Say, I have an idea."

"What's that?" I asked as I turned the yeast dough out onto the floured stainless steel counter.

"Let's have a competition. Whoever sells the most donuts this evening gets a reward."

"What did you have in mind? I'm not sure we can afford a cash prize, even with the added income we should take in tonight."

"I'm not talking about anything as crass as money," Emma said with a grin. "I was thinking more along the lines of sleep. The winner gets to come into the shop an hour late, or leave an hour early."

Since I was the boss, I felt an obligation to be the first one on the scene and the last one to turn off the lights as I was leaving, but Emma looked really eager to do this. "Sure. Why not? You've got a deal. I'll warn you right now that I'm not going to sleep in when I win. I'm going to take off at ten and let you close up the shop on your own."

"That's *if* you win, you mean," she said with a smile.

"Do I even need to ask which option you'll choose if you sell more than I do?" I asked her.

"I doubt it. I choose sleep—always sleep," she said.

As I worked on getting the yeast donuts ready, I smiled at the thought of the contest Emma had proposed. It might be a fun way to make the extra work pass by quickly. Neither one of us was going to get to see the movie, but that was okay with both of us. Since it was Momma's favorite, I'd already seen it a dozen times, and Emma hadn't shown any interest in seeing it alone since she was currently single again.

Hopefully, it would be an uneventful night, and we'd manage to raise some money for a worthwhile charity.

Unfortunately, that wasn't how it turned out at all.

CHAPTER 3

A LITTLE LATER, ONCE OUR ENTIRE inventory of donuts and drinks was ready, I realized that we still had an hour before we needed to start selling to the early birds that would surely gather to pick out the best spots by the park's gazebo where the backdrop for the movie would be set up. The gazebo had fallen into a state of disrepair lately, and since the town budget had already been stretched to its limit, there was talk of having a fundraiser for its restoration, but tonight's proceeds were going directly to feed the hungry, a worthier cause, at least in my mind. Tickets were a dollar apiece minimum, but most folks paid quite a bit more than that for the privilege of being chilly as they watched a movie together on an outdoor screen. Trish Granger, who owned the nearby Boxcar Grill, was donating half her profits to the cause as well, but she'd added another spin to things. She was charging a buck a head to use the restroom at the grill. There were porta-potties being supplied by the local contractor scattered all around the park, but I didn't know many folks who wouldn't spend a dollar for the comfort of using the diner's indoor facilities. Leave it to Trish to come up with a way to raise money for charity by using her restrooms. I would have done the same, but our bare facilities at the donut shop weren't open to the public.

"Why don't you take an hour off before we get started?" I suggested to Emma as she finished washing up the last dirty dish.

"Nice try, but I'm not falling for that, Suzanne," she said with a laugh.

"Falling for what?"

"You're going to start selling donuts the second I leave, aren't you?" she asked, grinning broadly as she did.

"Drats. You saw right through my nefarious scheme. What if I promise not to get started until you get back?"

"What are you going to do if I take a break?" she asked me.

"First, I'm going to clean up the sales cart. If there's time after that, I might go to the cottage and take a quick nap."

"Could you really fall asleep that fast?"

"Emma, the older I get, the more I appreciate a little snooze during the afternoon. Just wait. You'll see."

"I'll take your word for it," she said. "If you don't mind, I'll hang around and help you clean up the cart. The truth is, I'm not in any hurry to get home. Mom and Dad are squabbling again, and I'd just as soon not get in between them."

Emma's father, Ray Blake, owned and ran the town newspaper. He prided himself on being a genuine reporter, but his leads never turned out to be much. I hadn't realized that there was tension at home, though. "Is it serious?"

"No, not really. Dad's been complaining about all of the trips Mom has been planning. He threatened to go with her, but she called his bluff and invited him to go with her the next time; you know him. He won't leave that precious paper of his. It's just the same old verse, but I get tired of hearing it sometimes."

"Then let's get started on that cart," I said, feeling sorry for Emma's domestic situation but not knowing anything I could do about it. At one time, she and her best friend, Emily Hargraves, had talked about moving out of their parents' homes and sharing an apartment, but it sounded as though Emily and my ex-husband, Max, might be getting married any day, so Emily had pulled out of the deal. I was amazed how patient Max was being with Emily. They'd almost walked down the aisle together once, but murder had called off the nuptials. One of these days I figured they'd decide to elope, but in the meantime, they seemed perfectly content to share each other's company whenever they could manage it.

As we cleaned the cart up, several folks stopped by and asked about the donuts for sale inside. I looked at Emma and shrugged. "What do you think? Should we go ahead and open?"

"That depends. Who gets the sales?" she asked.

"Tell you what. If you start off working in the shop, I won't load the cart for an hour to give you a head start. Then, after my first hour, we'll switch off every hour until we're done for the night. After we're through, we can check our totals and see who gets the hour off we're battling for."

"How do we keep track of who sells what?" she asked.

"We'll use the honor system and keep a tally of what we each sell. I trust you. You trust me, don't you?" I asked her with a smile.

"Of course I do. After all, I know you wouldn't be able to live with a guilty conscience if you cheated," she said wickedly.

"Right back at you," I said. "Go on. Open up."

"It's a deal," she said as she invited the first inquiring customers in.

I had an hour to kill before I could start selling from the cart, so I decided that instead of taking a nap, I'd take a walk around town before things got busy.

Grace Gauge, my best friend, found me three minutes after I left the shop.

"Hey, Suzanne. Boy, you must be dead on your feet. Have you even been home today?"

"Barely," I said. "How about you? Are you finished for the day?"

She nodded as she grinned at me. "You know me. I get my work done fast. I think an eight-hour day at this point might actually kill me."

"As long as you can get away with it," I said. Grace was a sales supervisor at a cosmetics company, and she believed in a hands-off approach unless there were problems. It freed up a great deal of her day, and it offered the added bonus of making her employees all love her.

"Are you using the donut cart for movie night?" she asked as she pointed to our portable sales unit. "That's brilliant."

"Emma and I thought it might be fun having a competition to see who can sell the most donuts this evening."

"Then why aren't you stocked and selling? She's going to beat you at this rate."

There were three customers in the shop at the moment, so I really wasn't worried about it. "I'm good. Since I'm taking the first shift out here, I'm giving her a head start."

"What are you shooting for, a cash prize?"

"No, an hour off with pay," I admitted, feeling a little cheap with my offering. "Do you think that's enough?"

"Are you kidding? An hour of sleep is worth solid gold. Since you're not starting right away, do you want to take a walk? I'm headed over to the police station to give Stephen something."

"What's so important that you have to hand-deliver it?" I asked her.

"I bought him a raffle ticket from the Quilting Club. They're going to customize a quilt for the winner. Do you have your ticket yet?"

"I bought two," I admitted. "If I win, I'm going to have them make a donut-themed quilt for the shop."

"You're a woman of limited interests, aren't you?" she asked with a smile.

"What can I say? Donuts have become an obsession with me. Did you get a ticket for yourself?"

"I bought one, too," she admitted.

"What would yours feature?" I asked her.

"I haven't decided yet. I figure the odds are long of me winning, but since the proceeds are going to the Food Bank, how could I say no? I'm guessing that you're going to sell a lot of donuts tonight. Folks are really digging deep for this fundraiser."

"Why shouldn't they? I know that it's a cause near and dear to my heart," I said. We walked through town chatting about nothing in particular, but we didn't have to go all the way to the station to find the police chief. Stephen Grant was standing in front of city hall directing three volunteer firemen as they unloaded sixteen folding chairs from a pickup truck. They were for reserved seating up front, costing fifty dollars apiece, while everyone else had been encouraged to bring lawn chairs and blankets.

"Hey, babe. Got a second?" Grace asked him as we approached.

"In a minute," he said sternly, clearly unhappy about being called an endearment in front of the firefighters.

"Where should we set these up, ba...I mean Chief?" one of the firemen asked him with a devilish grin.

"Front and center, just like I said earlier," Chief Grant said sternly.

As the men were doing as they were told, the police chief said softly, "Come on, Grace. I have a tough enough time getting them to respect me without you adding to it. I'm younger than just about everybody in a position of authority around here."

"Sorry," she said, actually managing to look contrite for a moment. "I bought you a raffle ticket for the quilt drawing."

He managed to smile as he reached into his shirt pocket. "Great minds think alike. I got one for you, too."

"Let's trade," she said.

"Or, we could just keep the ones we bought," he said.

"No way, mister. That might ruin our luck," Grace said.

As they made the exchange, Stephen asked me, "Where's Jake?"

"He's in Raleigh visiting his sister," Grace answered before I could. "I told you about it."

"Oh, that's right. Sorry."

Was there a hint of pity in his voice as he said it? "There's nothing to be sorry about, Chief. He's visiting some of his family. I stayed behind to help Momma with all of this."

"By the way, where is your mother?" the chief asked me. "Have you seen her recently?"

"If I know her, she's getting George Morris ready for his presentation tonight. Gladys is the one she should be worried about, if you ask me."

"Why do you say that?"

"Think about it. She usually spends her days behind the scenes at the Boxcar Grill cooking. I'm not sure that she's ever spoken in public before."

"She's probably been coaching her as well," Chief Grant said. "Why does George need a pep talk?"

"The mayor is saying a few words about the Food Bank before the movie starts, and everybody knows he isn't that comfortable speaking in front of big crowds," I explained.

"It's an odd affliction for a politician to have," Grace said.

"Don't forget, Momma railroaded him into the job," I reminded her.

"Sure, the first time, but he ran for reelection and won handily since then. He can't really blame Dot for being in the job now."

"That's a point," I said.

Grace leaned in to kiss the chief's cheek, but he pulled away at the last second. "Come on, not in public," Chief Grant said.

Grace raised an eyebrow. "Seriously? Don't you think folks

around town know that we're together? Stephen Grant, if you don't kiss me right here and now in front of everyone, you're not going to get the opportunity to do it later in private."

The police chief took one glance at his girlfriend and saw that she wasn't kidding. He leaned in and gave her a hearty kiss, quite a bit more than the peck she'd just tried to deliver. When he pulled away, he asked, "Is that better?"

"Well, there's always room for improvement, but I'll give you a gold star for effort," she said with a wicked grin.

He just laughed, and then it faded quickly. "I cannot believe that they're putting the chairs in the wrong place. Excuse me, ladies. I've got to take care of this."

Once he walked over to join the firefighters, I said, "You were kind of hard on him, weren't you?"

"Hey, it takes a lot of effort to train a new boyfriend. He's more work than paper-training a puppy."

"I'll take your word for that," I said.

"Do you need any help with your donut cart sales?" Grace asked me a little later. "I can sell anything, from eyeliner to crullers. Just try me."

"I would, but I'm not sure that would be fair to Emma." I glanced at my watch and saw that it wouldn't be long until Momma started the festivities. It wasn't quite dark yet, but dusk was clearly on its way, and folks were beginning to gather in earnest. The screen, sections of plywood painted white, had been covered for days, and it would be pulled down only when the movie started. "Speaking of which, my hour is up. I'd better get busy selling."

"I'll see you after the movie," Grace said.

I walked into the donut shop and found Emma grinning. "Business has been booming. You're going to have to really hustle to catch up with me."

"Don't make any plans for that extra hour of sleep just yet," I answered as I started putting together three trays of our bestsellers. "Could you grab two urns and put some coffee in one and hot chocolate in the other? It's getting brisk out there," I said as I grabbed some paper cups.

"Are we counting coffee and cocoa sales, too?" Emma asked me.

"I thought we would. Would you like to exclude them and make it donuts only?"

"No, I think that's a great idea," she said, clearly trying to hide a smile.

"Let me guess. You've been selling lots of drinks, too."

"Maybe a little," she said, and then she laughed. "Or maybe even a little more than that."

"I'd better get busy, then," I said cheerfully. I didn't care if I won or not, but I was going to make it competitive if I could. I carried everything out and got busy selling.

I had the advantage of being mobile, and I planned on taking advantage of it.

A stranger approached and pointed to the urn labeled as coffee. "I'll take the biggest cup you've got," he said as he rubbed his hands together. He had a snaggletooth and a cowlick of black hair in front that looked to be untamable.

"Sorry, but it's just the one size tonight," I said.

"I'll take two, then," he said as he handed me a twenty-dollar bill. I filled his order and then started to make change. "You can keep that if you'll give me a little information," he said.

"I'm not sure that there's anything I can tell you that's worth that much," I said. The man was a puzzle for sure.

"Do you happen to know a fellow around seventy with a faded scar on one cheek? He probably has a beard and shaggy long hair, and I imagine he's quite a hermit. Does that ring any bells with you?"

It was a fit description of Gray Vincent, but I wasn't about to tell him that. There was something about him that I didn't like from the very start, and I'd learned over the years to trust my gut. I made the change and started to hand it to him, but he made no effort to take it. "Sorry. I can't imagine who you're talking about."

He frowned for a moment before he hid it. "My mistake. I thought I saw an old friend of mine in town the other day, but now I can't find him."

"What's his name?" I asked as I held onto the change momentarily. "That could help."

"Thanks, anyway," he said, blowing off my question and finally taking the offered change.

The entire exchange had been odd, but I quickly forgot it as I got busy selling donuts, coffee, and hot chocolate from my cart. I was still busy peddling goodies as Gladys and George took the impromptu stage together, with my mother between them. Momma tapped the mic three times, and that managed to get most folks' attention. She made a pair of quick introductions, and then she handed the microphone to the mayor. I continued working the crowd until Momma caught my eye. She was frowning at me, not that unusual a facial expression for her when it came to me, so I pulled the cart to the side and listened to George speak. After a few moments, he turned the mic over to Gladys, who spoke surprisingly eloquently about the Food Bank. I was proud of her for showing such poise under pressure. Hilda was by far the more outgoing of the two cooks Trish had on her staff, but Gladys was holding her own, maybe because she was so passionate about feeding those who couldn't afford a decent meal. As she spoke, I searched the crowd. It was overwhelmingly full of familiar faces, though there were a few strangers present, though still no sign of Gray. It was beginning to get dark now, and as Gladys wrapped up her comments, a motion from the back right side of the crowd caught my eye. Gray Vincent settled down on a lawn chair off to one side, characteristically alone. Something was clearly bothering him, but as I started toward him to see if I could help, Momma took the mic back from Gladys and said with a flourish, "Without further ado, we present *Dial M for Murder*."

The sheet came off the temporary screen, and the movie began to play, projected from somewhere in back.

I skirted toward the back of the crowd and pushed my cart over to where Gray was sitting, despite a few protests as I cut in front of a few of the viewers sitting even farther back.

"Gray, are you okay?" I asked him in a whisper.

"No, not really," he said, clearly worried about something. "Suzanne, I'm in trouble. I know you've dug into people's problems in the past. Would you and Grace be willing to help me?"

"Of course we will," I said, volunteering Grace's assistance without having to ask her. "Can you at least give me a hint what it's about?"

"Now's not the time. We'll talk after the show," he said.

I wanted to push him a little harder, but this wasn't the time or the place. After the show, we'd all have plenty of time to talk.

For now, I needed to trade places with Emma back at the shop.

I wasn't sure how many donuts I'd managed to sell during the event so far, but at least my total should be respectable when Emma and I compared numbers in the end.

She took over the cart, carrying her own cashbox, while I took over the empty shop. There was no use sitting around inside, so I watched part of the movie with Grace from the donut shop's front chairs. The angle was skewed, and the sound was tough to pick up, but it beat sitting on the ground, or even in a lawn chair. Trish must have made a killing on her restroom passes. It seemed to me that folks were constantly getting up and moving around, on their way to the restrooms mainly, but every now and then someone would join us and I'd have to stop to sell a donut or two and maybe some coffee or hot chocolate to go with them as well. I ended up catching bits and pieces of the movie as it played, not the best way to watch it by any means, but most of the folks who were attending the screening seemed to enjoy it.

I had no idea where Emma and I stood as the movie played, but it turned out to be the last thing on my mind when the film finally finished.

That was when things really began to fall apart.

CHAPTER 4

I KNEW THAT I NEEDED TO talk to Gray, but I had a few things that I had to do first. Emma and I unloaded the cart and the urns, and I was pushing the rig back to my rental building when I noticed that though Gray's lawn chair was still there, the man himself was gone. Had he slipped off to use the restroom? I waited a few minutes, but when he didn't return, I decided to check things out.

On top of his chair, I found a folded piece of paper, one that had obviously been torn out of a small notebook and left there for someone to find.

It was addressed to me.

"Suzanne, I couldn't stay. Bring Grace out to my place as soon as you read this, no matter how late it might be. The gate will be unlocked. Hurry."

I frowned as I folded the note up and stuck it in my jeans pocket. I needed to find Grace, and as soon as I stowed the cart, I made that my mission.

As I was looking for her, Emma came up, smiling. "I hope you brought your best stuff, because I made a killing tonight."

It took me a second to realize what she was talking about. "Oh. The bet. You win. You can take your hour whenever you'd like to."

"Suzanne, what's wrong?" she asked. It was obvious that something was troubling me, or I never would have conceded the friendly competition so easily.

"Have you seen Grace around? She was just here."

"She's over there talking to the chief," Emma said as she pointed.

"Great. Do you mind locking up? I have something I need to do."

"Don't you want to cash out the day's receipts and figure out how much we're donating to the Food Bank?" Emma asked.

I'd completely forgotten about the money we'd made tonight. "Would you mind doing it?"

"Not at all. I'm happy to. Suzanne, something is clearly wrong, so don't bother trying to deny it. The question is, can I help?"

I touched her shoulder lightly. "You are. Thanks for everything tonight. That was above and beyond the call of duty."

"It was my pleasure. I don't know if I told you, but last semester I wrote a paper for class about the problems of the poor here at home, and it really shook me up. Did you know that most folks are two paychecks away from being homeless, and a great many of them don't have enough to eat? I feel bad enough for the adults, but the kids are the ones who are really suffering. We've got to do something."

I smiled at her. "We are. Sometimes I forget what a big heart you have."

"It's the same size as everyone else's," she said, trying to downplay the compliment.

"We both know better than that. Thanks for taking care of things at the shop."

"Happy to do it. You'd better go catch her. It looks as though she's leaving."

I glanced over and saw that she was right. Grace was heading home, and I needed to stop her before she got there. "Grace. Grace! Hang on!"

The second, louder, shout caught her attention. She turned

around and started back toward me. "What's up, Suzanne? Do you need something?"

"We need to go to Gray's cabin," I said.

"Now? Seriously? What makes you think he's going to let us in?"

I pulled the note from my pocket and handed it to her. It was easier than trying to explain it to her. In the dim light coming from the street lamp, she read it in silence, and after two seconds, she nodded and handed it back to me. "I'd better tell Stephen what we're up to, and then we can go. We're taking your Jeep, I assume."

"If you don't mind," I said. "Who knows what the road to the cabin is like once we get past the gate? You don't want to take any chances with your company car, do you?"

"No, ma'am, I do not. I'll meet you at the donut shop in one minute."

"Thanks for allowing me to volunteer your services," I said as she started to leave.

"Are you kidding? I would have been upset with you if you hadn't. I'm not celebrating the fact that Jake is out of town, but it's going to be kind of nice doing something important and mysterious with just you again."

"What makes you think it's going to be either one of those things?" I asked her.

"Really? How can it not be? You have to admit that whenever we get together, trouble never seems to be very far away."

"For once, I hope you're wrong," I replied.

"I do, too, but neither one of us thinks I am, do we?"

"No. I've got a feeling something bad is going on with Gray Vincent. I just hope we can help."

"There's only one way to find out."

"What do you think is really going on with him?" Grace asked me as we drove to Gray's cabin in the woods. It was full-on dark now, and quite a bit past my bedtime, but I wasn't at all sleepy. Maybe it was the adrenaline rush about what we might soon learn at Gray's place.

As promised, the gate was unlocked, though it had still been pulled shut.

"Do you want me to get it?" Grace asked.

"No, I don't mind," I said as I put my Jeep into park, got out, swung the gate open, and then got back in.

As I drove through, Grace asked, "Should we close it back behind us?"

"I don't see why we should. After all, we won't be here all night, and we'll just have to open it again to get back out later."

"We hope," she said. "I just realized something. If this takes too long, you're not even going to get a nap before it's time to make donuts again."

I glanced at my watch and knew that she was right. I'd gone two days without sleep before, but it was never anything I embraced willingly. The older I got, the less I was able to stay awake for extended periods of time. I didn't have much choice now, but I did find myself wishing I'd taken that nap earlier when I'd had the chance.

There was a source of light up ahead, and as we took the last bend of the rough road before we got to the cabin, I realized that Gray had left the outside lights on for us. I'm not sure what I was expecting, but it certainly wasn't what we found. The place was a wonderland, landscaped beautifully with plantings, paths, lanterns, and a host of too much to take in with one glance. A series of precious little fairy houses were spread throughout the plantings, making the place look as though it were ready for a photo shoot for a gardening magazine. I was beginning to see what Gray did out there all by himself during the day.

"This place is absolutely magical," Grace said. "Are you seeing the same thing I am?"

"I can hardly believe it, myself," I said as I swung the Jeep toward the parking pad. Gray's battered old truck was there, and I wedged my Jeep in beside it.

As I did, I caught a glimpse of an odd feature that I hadn't noticed earlier.

There was a scarecrow with its back to us, looking out into the woods.

Why would Gray need a scarecrow there, particularly at this time of the year?

Then I realized that it was no scarecrow.

There was a man pinned against a wrought-iron trellis, his arms extended as if to welcome the woodland creatures to this bit of tortured paradise.

CHAPTER 5

I JERKED THE JEEP TO A halt.

"Suzanne, what are you doing?" Grace asked me as I jumped out and ran toward what I'd just seen.

"That's not a scarecrow!" I said as I raced to the figure. Maybe I was wrong. It might not be a man, I kept telling myself, but I knew in my heart that I was wrong.

It was Gray, and the moment I saw his whitened face and his bloody chest, I knew that we were too late.

"Who would do this?" I asked her, sobbing as I fought to untie him, though I knew that Gray Vincent was long past caring.

Grace finally managed to pull me away. "Suzanne! Stop!"

"We can't just leave him like that," I said through my tears.

She grabbed my shoulders and physically stopped me. It shocked me just how much stronger she was than I was at that moment. "We don't have any choice. Stephen needs to see this."

I took a deep breath, and the madness I'd been feeling was suddenly gone. "You're right. Of course you're right. I'm okay. Thanks."

"You're welcome. Now, why don't you walk back over to the Jeep while I call Stephen?"

"I'll be fine right here," I said. I couldn't look directly at the body anymore, so I kept my gaze focused out into the woods. Beyond the lights Gray had set up, there was nothing but darkness. Still, I couldn't shake the feeling that someone was watching us from the forest, even though I knew that it was most likely just my imagination. Who would kill this harmless old man? Had they done it before they'd strung him up, or after? For some reason it was important to me to know, though I might not ever find out the answer. I couldn't have said what Grace told the chief of police, but the next thing I knew, he and a full crew of his deputies were on the scene. Grace took my arm in hers, and we walked unsteadily back to the Jeep.

After giving the scene a preliminary look, Chief Grant joined us a few minutes later. He looked into my eyes. "Suzanne, are you okay?"

"I'm fine," I said. We both knew that I was lying, but it didn't seem to matter. I thought I'd been hardened to seeing things like what we'd just found, but clearly I'd been wrong.

"Sure you are. Tell me what happened."

"Can't this wait, Stephen?" Grace asked him. "I need to get her home."

"I'm sorry, but what she knows could be important to my investigation," the chief said, clearly unhappy about having to cross his girlfriend.

"It's okay," I said. "I need to tell him."

Grace nodded, and then she put her arm around my waist, though I couldn't say whether it was to offer her support or simply to steady me so I didn't fall over.

"I spoke with Gray right before the movie. He was clearly upset about something, so I went over to check on him. He asked me for our help, but when I found his lawn chair after the movie, he was already gone. All he left behind was a note for us to come out here as soon as we could. We did as he asked, and we found him like that," I said, trying not to glance over at where the body was still tethered. "Do you have to leave him like that? Why doesn't someone at least cut him down?"

"We have to wait for the medical examiner," Chief Grant said calmly. "It shouldn't be long."

I wanted to protest that it was undignified leaving him so vulnerable, but then I realized how foolish I was being. Gray was long past caring, so why should I be so upset by it?

"And you don't have any idea what he wanted to discuss with you?" the chief asked me.

"I don't have a clue," I admitted.

"Okay. May I see the note?"

I pulled it out of my pocket and handed it to him, but he wouldn't take it directly. "It's okay. Gray left it for me. Nobody else's fingerprints are going to be on it."

"That's entirely possible, but we can't be too careful," he said as pulled an evidence bag from his pants pocket and had me place the note inside. After he sealed it up, he studied it for a moment, and then the chief turned back to me. "Is this Gray's handwriting?"

"I have no idea. I just naturally assumed that it was." The thought that someone else might have left that note for me hadn't even crossed my mind. Was the chief onto something, or was he just being overly paranoid?

"We'll find out. Is that all you know?"

"Yes. No. Maybe," I said.

"Stephen, can't you see she's in shock? I need to get her home," Grace insisted. "Suzanne, give me your keys. I'm driving."

I was so numb that I actually handed them over. Grace had never driven my Jeep before in her life, and I was a tad overprotective of it, despite its age and general rough condition.

"Hang on a second. We're not finished here yet," Chief Grant told her, and Grace nodded once.

"You have thirty seconds, and then I'm getting her out of here, whether you like it or not."

He shrugged, not in agreement, but not opposing her, either. "Suzanne, you were about to tell me something."

"It's probably nothing," I said.

"Tell me anyway."

"This afternoon, I saw Gray near the city hall. He looked haunted by someone or something. When I turned around, I could swear I saw someone ducking behind the other side of the building, but when I got there, whoever it was that might have been following him was gone."

"Do you have any idea of who it might have been?"

"She would have said so if she had, don't you think?" Grace asked crossly.

"Bear with me for just one more minute," the chief said. "Any impressions at all? Man or woman? Young or old? Anything you might remember could help us find his killer."

I searched my memories to see if I could answer his questions, but I kept drawing a blank. "I'm sorry. I don't know who it was."

The chief nodded. "It's okay. You've had quite a shock. Both of you have," he added, including Grace with a soft smile.

She didn't respond in kind. It was as though she were a mother lion looking after one of her kittens.

The chief frowned for a moment, but then he continued, "If you think of something later, call me, day or night, okay?"

"Okay," I said. "There's one other thing."

"What's that?" he asked eagerly.

"I ran into a man before the movie who described Gray and asked if I knew where he could find him. It struck me as a little odd at the time, but I forgot all about it until now."

"Tell me about him," the chief said.

After I gave him a general description of the man, I said,

"There was something about him that I didn't like. I didn't tell him a thing, and he didn't linger."

"Could he have been the same person following Gray earlier?" the chief asked.

"I couldn't say. I'm sorry. That's really all that I know."

"Thanks. We'll see if we can track him down," he said as he closed up his notebook.

"Come on, Suzanne. I'm getting you home," Grace said. It was clear there was no overruling her this time. It felt odd getting into the Jeep's passenger side. Jake usually didn't even drive my Jeep, but I wasn't in any shape to put up a fight.

As Grace drove, I asked, "Why aren't you as shaken as I am by what we found out there?"

"Believe me, at the first opportunity I get, I plan on collapsing into a ball of mush. Right now, I have to be strong for you. I didn't try to get him down; in fact, I didn't even touch him. You're the one who had the guts to check for a pulse."

"For all of the good it did him," I said, remembering with a shudder the feeling of Gray's dead skin as I'd searched for any sign of life.

"At least you tried. That's what counts," she said. "You should close the donut shop tomorrow. You need your rest."

"Funny, I was thinking just the opposite. I've got a feeling that I'm going to be needing the shop to take my mind off what we just saw."

"Will you at least be able to get a nap before you have to start making donuts? You've got four hours before you need to get to work. It's not much, but it might help."

"Grace, I can't imagine going to sleep tonight after what we just saw. Can you?"

"No," she quickly admitted. "We could always watch a movie at your place, since Jake's gone."

"You don't have to babysit me," I said, though the idea of having her company actually lightened my heart a little.

"How do you know I'm not doing it as much for me as I am for you?" she asked me with a grin.

"I don't," I answered. "Okay. We'll make it a party. Strike that. There's not going to be anything festive about it, but I wouldn't say no to having you at the cottage with me."

"And there's no place on earth I'd rather be," she said as she reached over and patted my knee.

We settled in on the couch back home and put a movie in the DVD player. At least we'd have each other for company until it was time for me to go to work again.

The truth was that the opening credits hadn't even finished rolling before I found myself drifting off to sleep. The strain of the current events had clearly taken more out of me than I could have imagined.

The next thing I knew, my internal alarm clock was waking me up.

It was time to make the donuts again.

I glanced over at Grace, but she was sound asleep herself, and I didn't have the heart to wake her. I got up as quietly as I could manage, got ready for work, and left her a note before I took off, flashing back for an instant to the one I'd gotten from the recently dead man.

To my surprise, there were lights on at the donut shop when I got there.

Had Emma decided to show up early, or was someone else paying me a visit?

I thought about calling Chief Grant, but when I looked through the front window, I saw that everything appeared to be intact, and to my surprise, Emma's coat was hanging up on the rack.

CHAPTER 6

"E MMA, I THOUGHT FOR SURE that you would be sleeping in today. After all, you won the bet last night, fair and square."

"Honestly, after what you went through last night, I didn't think you'd be coming in today," she admitted. Emma was washing the last of the dishes from the night before, but at least she hadn't started on the day's cake donuts yet. "Dad told me what happened at Gray's. I'm so sorry you had to go through that."

"It was pretty horrible," I admitted. It didn't surprise me that Ray had heard about Gray's murder. I didn't doubt that he had a source on the police force, but if Stephen Grant ever found the leak, one deputy was going to be out of a job on the spot. "You shouldn't have come in," I said as I took my own coat off and put it beside Emma's.

"But you're glad that I did, right?" she asked with a grin.

"More than you'll ever know. The truth is, I don't know what I'd do without you."

"No worries on that count. You won't have to find out anytime soon," Emma said. She had left me briefly once to go away to college, but she'd quickly come back home. I knew that her time of employment at the shop wouldn't last forever, but I'd take every minute I could get until it was time for her to move on permanently. "I should have figured that you'd be here right on schedule, come what may."

"Sometimes it's the only thing in my life that makes sense," I said as I started accumulating the ingredients I'd need to make the cake donuts. Running the donut shop required two different sets of skills for donutmaking. The cake donuts were made using one method, while the raised yeast donuts were something altogether different. I didn't mind, though. I enjoyed both processes more than the actual selling, though it was usually a pleasure seeing my customers too—many of them my friends—every day.

I'd been right. The work helped take my mind off of what I'd seen just a few short hours before. Soon enough, it was nearing time for our break. As Emma and I walked outside the donut shop in the darkness, I saw a police cruiser head up Springs Drive toward us. At least the lights and siren were off.

Who could be paying us a visit this time of morning? To my surprise, it was Chief Grant himself.

As he got out of the squad car, I asked him, "Have you been up all night?"

"So far," he said with a shrug. "Right now I'm going home for a quick nap, and then I'll be back at my desk before dawn."

"We have fresh cake donuts and hot coffee inside," I offered. "You're welcome to whatever we have."

"I'll skip the coffee, but I wouldn't mind a donut or two," he admitted.

"What kind would you like?"

"Plain cake will be fine," he said, and then he turned to my assistant. "Emma, would you mind grabbing me a couple for the road? And take your time. I need a few minutes with Suzanne."

"Of course," my assistant said, and she quickly disappeared back inside.

"What's up, Chief?" I asked him.

"It's about earlier."

"What about it?" I asked. I'd been trying to get rid of the image of Gray tied to that trellis since I'd first seen it, but it just wouldn't go away.

"I'm sorry if I was a little abrupt with you at the crime scene," he said softly.

"You were just doing your job," I replied. "Did Grace put you up to coming by and apologizing to me?"

"No, but I know what she's going to say the second I see her, so I thought I'd fire a preemptive strike by coming by to see you first. This way, it makes it look as though it was my idea, and not hers."

"Sorry about that. She's a little overprotective of me."

"You don't have to tell me that," the chief said, and for a moment he looked his age. It vanished just as quickly as it had appeared, though, and the police chief was quickly back. "Anyway, I shouldn't have been so hard on you."

"No worries," I said with a smile. "I appreciate the gesture, though. Do you have any idea why someone would want to kill Gray Vincent?"

"I'm afraid it's a little more complicated than that."

"How so?"

"I don't suppose there's any reason to keep it a secret, though if you could keep it to yourself for a few hours, I'd greatly appreciate it."

"You know you can trust me. What's up?"

"The truth of the matter is, Gray Vincent doesn't exist."

"What are you talking about? I know, knew, the man personally." Had the police chief bumped his head at some point this evening? Or was it possible he was simply sleep deprived?

"You saw someone who'd been recently murdered, but his name wasn't Gray Vincent."

"Chief, Gray has been coming into my shop since I first took over, and he hasn't missed ten days since. I know him nearly as well as I know you."

"You might think so. I knew a man going by the name of Gray Vincent as well, but it turns out that he's just someone's fabrication. All of it is fake: his driver's license, birth certificate, social security number, all of it. A week before he came to April Springs, a man about our mysterious friend's age died suddenly, and Gray took over his identity. We don't know who he is, but it's dead certain that he's not Gray Vincent, or wasn't, at any rate."

"I can't believe it," I said.

"I'm having a little trouble swallowing it myself," the chief said. "We're running his prints with the feds, but it takes a while. Right now, we're looking for a killer. I have a feeling Gray's identity may have something to do with why he was murdered, but we won't know that right away, so we're doing the best we can with what we've got. I don't even know what to call him. I opened the case as Gray Vincent, but now I know that's not true. I can't stand the thought of putting John Doe on the file; whatever the man's name was, we knew him for a long time."

"You do what you want; I'm going to keep calling him Gray," I said, wondering about the story he'd told me about his name. It had been a clever way of explaining the oddity of it. I was pretty sure that he would have liked a more generic name to start his new life with, but it couldn't be that easy coming up with one from someone who'd been recently deceased.

"I know. It feels right, doesn't it? I'm not going to sit around and wait for proper identification. It's still a homicide committed in my jurisdiction, so that makes it mine, and I plan on finding out who did it. Have you had any luck remembering anything else? The truth of the matter is that right now, I'm grasping at straws."

"Was there nothing in his cabin that helped?" I asked.

"No, it looked as though he could have walked away from it at a moment's notice. There weren't any personal photos, documents, or anything that might help figure this out. I'm stumped."

"I'm just sorry I can't help. I've been trying to come up with anything that might shed a little light on the situation, but I'm drawing a complete blank myself. I think I'm still in shock."

"To be honest, I was surprised to find you working this morning," he said.

"There's no place I'd rather be. By the way, Grace is sleeping on my couch. Neither one of us thought we'd be able to rest, so we popped in a movie. The next thing I knew I was waking up at my regular time, and Grace was snoring softly beside me. I didn't have the heart to wake her up."

"She was worn out by the ordeal, too," he said. "Are you two thinking about diving into this case?"

"We don't have much choice," I said honestly. "It was bad enough that he asked us for our help and we couldn't provide it, but finding him like that makes it even more personal."

"I get it, but you know I can't sanction your investigation," he said gravely.

I smiled at him. "I would have been shocked if you did. We'll do our best to stay out of your way."

"I've got to admit that I could use some help on this one. If Jake were in town, I'd try to deputize him."

My husband would have readily accepted the assignment; I knew that without even asking. "Sorry, but you're stuck with Grace and me this time."

"I'm not underestimating your abilities to get folks around here to talk to you. I knew it as a cop, and even more so as the police chief, that a lot of people in April Springs are reticent to share anything with members of law enforcement."

"While a donut lady and a makeup saleswoman are completely harmless," I said with a laugh.

"Don't forget who you're talking to. I know for a fact that

you two are about as harmless as a pair of copperheads," he said, unguarded words springing from his exhaustion. "No offense intended."

"Are you kidding? That's a compliment, and I know it. We'll stay out from underfoot, but we can still poke around the edges and see if there's anything we can find out from our end of things. If we do, I promise that we'll come straight to you with it." It was a fairly new concession on my part, but if it helped the chief of police give us a little leeway in our investigations, it was worth it.

"Fair enough," he said as he motioned to Emma. She'd been standing by the front counter watching us, for how long I didn't have a clue.

"You called?" she asked as she joined us.

As Chief Grant handed her a pair of singles and a quarter to cover the tax, he said, "Thanks."

"You've got a little change coming back from this," Emma said.

"Save it for the next guy who comes in a little short," the chief said.

"Will do," she said, and then he got into the car and drove off.

"What was that all about?" Emma asked me after the police chief was gone.

I'd promised not to say anything just yet, and though I believed I could trust Emma, I wasn't entirely sure she'd be able to withstand the temptation of telling her father the blockbuster news about Gray. "He came by to apologize for something that happened earlier." It was true, too. It just wasn't the complete story.

"That's sweet. Did Grace put him up to it?" Emma asked with a mischievous grin.

"No, evidently he came forward all on his own."

She was about to ask me something else when the timer went off. I was, quite literally, saved by the bell.

"Time to get busy making more donuts," I said, and we walked back into the shop together.

I was going to have to talk with Grace about what had just happened, but it would have to wait for now. Not only was she most likely still asleep, but I had other things to do at the moment, like take the dough I had waiting for me and transform it all into delicious donuts to share with anyone in April Springs who had a yen for a sweet treat this morning.

CHAPTER 7

F IVE MINUTES BEFORE WE WERE set to open for the day, my cellphone rang.

It was Jake.

I slid the last tray of donuts into the display case and took the call.

"Hey, Jake. How are Sarah and the kids?"

"Not great," he said, and I could hear the exhaustion in his voice. "My sister has gotten herself tangled up with yet another bad boy, and I'm trying to break her free."

Sarah had a habit of going for the worst possible men she could find, something that had a negative impact on her kids. It was one of the reasons Jake had paid so much more attention to them than he had his other nieces and nephews.

"Why does she keep doing that to herself?" I'd never understood the impulse to date guys who were trouble, if you excluded Tommy Thorndike in the sixth grade. Then again, Tommy and I had dated again a little in high school, and if anyone in our class had been destined for trouble, it had been Tommy. I'd known in my heart that I couldn't change him, but I quickly saw the folly in even trying. He'd disappeared just before graduation, and I hadn't heard from him since. For all I knew, he was in Raleigh dating Sarah now, but somehow I doubted it.

"She swears that she's going to change as soon as she's free of this one, but I've heard that before," Jake said. "We'll see.

In the meantime, do you mind if I extend my stay here a little while longer?"

"No, of course not. Take all the time you need." I felt a little selfish letting Jake stay in Raleigh without me, but I had my reasons. If he were home, it would be twice as tough investigating what had happened to Gray with Grace. I loved my husband dearly, but he was still having a tough time getting used to the fact that I was a decent investigator myself.

"Okay, that was a little too easy," he said softly. "Suzanne, what's going on there?"

I couldn't even lie to the man by omission, not that I tried, but maybe I could postpone telling him the truth until Grace and I could get started. "I don't know what you're talking about. I have my work in April Springs, and you're needed there. It just makes sense."

After a long pause, he said, "At least I know there's not someone else. After what Max did to you, you'd never cheat on me; you'd cut me loose first. You're not getting tired of me, are you?"

The poor dear. There was a real air of concern in his voice. I had to tell him the truth to ease his fears, no matter what the consequences might be for our investigation. "Of course not. There's been a bit of trouble here. That's all."

"What happened?" It was his "cop-voice," one I well recognized.

"First off, I'm not in any danger," I said quickly.

"Okay, I don't like the way this is going. Why don't you just lay it out for me, and I'll be the judge of that?"

"I'd be happy to, but I'm opening the donut shop in three minutes," I said. "I don't have a whole lot of time."

"Fine. You can tell me when I get there. I'll see you in three and a half hours."

"Hold on. I'll find the time," I said quickly before he could hang up and put his plan into action. I knew my husband. If we left things as they were, there would be no dissuading him from joining me, no matter how much trouble his sister might be in. "Gray Vincent was murdered last night."

"Gray? Who would want to kill that old hermit?" Jake asked.

"Nobody can figure that out just yet," I said.

"He was a steady customer of yours, wasn't he?"

I nodded, forgetting for one second that Jake couldn't see me. "Yes, he was one of my regulars. Gray was an odd bird, but I liked him."

"Is that why you feel obligated to dig into what happened to him?" my husband asked me.

"Does that surprise you?" I asked him, holding back the fact that Gray and I had interacted the day before, and furthermore, that he'd asked me for my help.

"No, but there's more to it than that. I just know it."

How did he do that? Could the man read my mind, or was I that transparent? "I spoke to him before the movie started last night. He told me he was in trouble, and he asked me if Grace and I might be able to help."

"What kind of trouble was he in?"

"That's what we were hoping to find out. We were supposed to meet up with him after the movie, but he was already gone. He left a note on his chair for us to meet him at his house, so Grace and I drove out there, but we were too late. He was already dead."

"How did it happen?" Jake asked softly.

"It was bad. Somebody tied him up to a wrought-iron trellis and stabbed him in the chest."

"How many times was he stabbed?"

"Just once, as near as I could tell. Why?"

There was silence on the other end for a few moments, and I knew that Jake's cop brain was analyzing the information. "It doesn't make sense."

"I know. That's why Grace and I are going to do a little digging on the side. Chief Grant came by the donut shop during our break earlier and told me that he didn't mind if Grace and I snooped around a little. Oh, there's something else that you should know."

"I'm listening."

"It appears that the man we all knew as Gray Vincent was a fabrication. He stole the name off of a dead man. Nobody knows who he really was at this point."

"Has Grant run his prints?" I heard Jake sigh slightly on the other end.

"It's being done even as we speak. Listen, there's nothing to worry about from my end. Grace and I are going to see if we can make a list of the folks who might have known about Gray's secret. There's no need to worry, though. We're not actively looking for a killer."

"Unless someone in town did it," Jake said. "I still don't like it."

"Which part?" I asked.

"The part where you and Grace risk your lives digging into a homicide," he answered immediately.

"Let me ask you something. Do you honestly think that you'd be able to dissuade us if you were standing right here in front of me? The man asked me for my help, and I couldn't manage to do it before someone killed him."

"Because you never got the chance," Jake snapped.

"That doesn't change anything, and you know it." I had a stubborn streak a mile wide at times, and my husband was well aware of it.

"I could at least be there as backup for you," he offered softly.

"When your sister needs you there so desperately? Sweetheart, I appreciate the offer, and if things get dicey, I'll call you, but Grace and I can handle this." I just hoped that I was convincing.

I had one more minute until the shop was set to open, and a few folks were already outside waiting to get in. Since I'd cut back on my hours of operation, I'd found that it had increased foot traffic, not limited it. People were odd, but I wasn't complaining. Working less for more money was a situation I could happily find a way to live with.

"I still don't like it," he finally said.

"We'll be careful," I promised.

"And you'll honestly tell me if you're in trouble?" he asked, clearly not believing me, not that I could blame him, based on my past performance.

"I promise. Stay right where you are."

"I will, but I want hourly updates," he said flatly.

I laughed at the suggestion. "We both know that's not going to happen."

He joined me in my laughter, and I was happy we'd been able to interject a little humor into the situation. "What can I say? It was worth a shot. How about twice a day?"

"I'll bring you up to speed before I go to bed every night. That's the most I can promise and follow through on. What do you say? Do we have a deal?"

"Why do I suddenly feel as though I'm buying a used truck?" he asked with a soft chuckle.

"I'm worth a great deal more than that, or you married the wrong woman."

"There are things in my life that I'm not sure of, but that will never be one of them," he said, and I felt the truth permeate his voice. I was so happy that we'd found each other, for the millionth time for the thousandth reason.

"Now, I'd love to stay on the line and chat, but I've got donuts to sell. That call was good timing, by the way."

"I knew it was the one time of day that I'd be sure to catch you," he said. "Will it hurt if I tell you to be careful, Suzanne?"

"That never hurts," I said. "Good luck with Sarah and her situation."

"Thanks. I'm afraid that I'm going to need it."

"My, but don't we lead interesting lives?"

"As long as we're together, in spirit if not in fact, then I'm okay with everything else," he said.

It was a sweet way to sign off, and I found myself smiling as I went to the door and unlocked it.

The smile didn't have much time to exist.

One of my early visitors was not my biggest fan, and the feeling was most assuredly mutual. Over the years we'd found ways to get along, but it was always a trying experience.

What on earth was Gabby Williams doing at the donut shop, especially this early in the morning?

"Hey, Gabby. Fancy seeing you here. What happened, did you get a craving for a donut all of a sudden?" I asked her as she made her way to the counter. She was a stylish woman who owned the gently used clothing store, ReNEWed—which happened to be next door to me—but she didn't often come by Donut Hearts for donuts. As a matter of fact, not ever, at least not since one of my customers had pelted her shop with heavily iced treats.

"I'm not here for your tasty little death-bombs, Suzanne."

"So, you admit that they are tasty," I said with a hint of a smile. Any broader, and it would make Gabby dig her heels in, and I might never learn why she was really there. It was a fine line I was dancing, but I'd done it with her before.

"It's about Gray Vincent," she said softly and solemnly.

That took the wind out of my sails immediately. "What about him?"

"Do you really want to discuss it out here in front of

everyone?" There were half a dozen customers in the shop, with more heading our way.

I shook my head. "I do not. Let's go into the kitchen."

She looked in that general direction with clear distaste. "I'd rather do this outside, if you don't mind. I have no desire to see how the sausage is made."

"Making donuts is a lot prettier than that," I said, but I wasn't going to push the point. "I'll meet you out front in thirty seconds."

"If it's thirty-one, I'm leaving," she said as she exited the building.

I knew that it wasn't hyperbole, either; Gabby usually meant what she said.

I found Emma in the kitchen, up to her elbows in soapy water. She was singing along with whatever was playing on her iPod, and I had to tap her on the shoulder to get her attention. "Can you watch the front for a few minutes?"

"Absolutely," she said as she rinsed off her hands. Once upon a time she'd been reluctant to interact with our customers directly, but lately she'd been coming into her own, easy and confident after assuming my duties far too many times recently.

"I shouldn't be long," I said.

"Take your time."

As I headed for the front door, I saw Gabby walking away.

Blast that woman, if she weren't so useful to me, I would have let her storm off, but unfortunately, I wasn't in any position to turn down any help I might be able to get.

"Hang on," I said breathlessly as I burst outside. "According to my watch, I made it in time." That was an outright lie, but I decided to own it. Besides, Gabby wouldn't have come to the shop if she didn't have something worth sharing. The woman loved knowing things that other folks didn't, and she rarely passed up the opportunity to hold that over me.

"Barely," Gabby said reluctantly. "I heard that you were the one who found Gray's body last night. Is that true?"

"It is," I said, not being able to stop myself from shivering a little at the memory.

"It must have been awful for you," she said sympathetically.

"I've had better nights in my life," I admitted.

"Does that mean that you and Grace are going to investigate?" she asked me, piercing me with her gaze.

"I know you think we're crazy to do it, but honestly, do we have any choice? You don't happen to know why we were there in the first place, do you?"

Gabby frowned, clearly unhappy about not knowing something that I did, for a change of pace. "No. Now that you mention it, Gray was notorious about his privacy. Why were you and Grace there in the middle of the night?"

"He asked us for our help, but before we could offer him the least bit of assistance, somebody killed him."

The information rocked Gabby back on her heels. "You're right. You really don't have any choice, do you?" Her confirmation of our motivation surprised me. There was always more to this woman than I realized, and she rarely failed to do something that made me reevaluate my opinion of her on a fairly regular basis.

"We don't think so," I agreed. "What do you know about Gray?"

"If you're asking if I know why someone would want to kill that harmless old man, I'm afraid that I can't help you."

Frankly, I was disappointed with the answer. "I was kind of hoping that's why you were here."

"I may not know who the killer might be, but that doesn't mean that I still can't be useful to you," Gabby said. "Someone we both know rather well was closer to Gray than anyone in town realizes. She might be able to help you."

"Don't keep me hanging. Who exactly are you talking about?"

I thought Gabby was going to hold onto the name a little longer, but she must have seen the desperation in my eyes. "Suzanne, you and Grace need to speak with Gladys Murphy."

"*Trish's* Gladys?" I asked. Gladys's name was a surprise to me. She was fairly good behind the grill, though not as good as Hilda Fremont, but to be fair, not many people were. "What has she got to do with this mess?"

"She's been dating Gray recently," Gabby said. The gleam in her eye about knowing something that I didn't was back where it belonged.

"I don't believe it," I said flatly.

Gabby looked at me sharply. "You're not doubting my word, are you?"

"Of course not," I said quickly. I knew better than to offend Gabby when it came to the information she shared. It was rarely, if ever, wrong, though usually not so freely given. "I just never put them together."

"Why do you think he came out to Movie Night in the first place?" Gabby asked. "From what I gather, he and Gladys just broke up, and it was bad on both sides."

"You're not suggesting that *Gladys* killed him, are you?" I asked, dumbfounded by the mere thought of it.

"I'm not suggesting anything of the sort!" Gabby snapped. "I'm just saying that if you're looking for insights into the man's life, Gladys is the person you should be talking to. She's working the lunch shift at the Boxcar today, but if you get to her before eleven, then she might be able to help. I happen to know that she sits in the park for a half hour, rain or shine, before every shift."

"How can you possibly know that?" I asked.

"I've seen her out there countless times, as I'm sure you have yourself."

I had, but I hadn't put it together with her work schedule

at the Boxcar Grill. "But I don't close the shop until eleven," I protested.

"Suzanne, I'm not here to make your life easier," Gabby said, which was true on so many levels. "The logistics of your investigation are up to you. I just thought you might be able to use the information."

"I do, and I greatly appreciate it," I said. "How do you happen to know Gladys's schedule?"

"My dear girl, you should know by now that there's little that goes on in April Springs that I *don't* know," Gabby said, trying to sound mysterious.

The problem was that it was true.

Gabby had sources I could only dream of. I liked to pride myself on the fact that I had my finger on the pulse of our quaint little town, but Gabby was the true operator among us. "Thanks."

"My pleasure," she said. "I hope you catch whoever did this. I liked Gray Vincent."

"Romantically?" I asked, regretting the question as soon as it left my lips.

"Don't be ridiculous," Gabby said, and then, without another word, she walked to her shop.

I was going to have to get Emma to cover for me for the half hour before we closed. This was too good of an opportunity to pass up.

As I went back into Donut Hearts, I couldn't imagine the conversation I'd be having with Gladys in a few hours, but at least I had some time to prepare myself for it.

CHAPTER 8

I COULD BARELY CONTAIN MYSELF UNTIL it would be time to leave the donut shop to speak with Gladys, but it wasn't time just yet, and I had a real job to perform at Donut Hearts. I knew I wasn't exactly saving lives by selling donuts, but the world was a happier place with me in it than not, and I could live with that. I arranged with Emma to take over at ten thirty, but I hadn't been able to track Grace down as of yet. I would have loved it if she could be with me when I spoke to Gladys, but if I had to, I'd do it without her.

After a rather full morning of dodging questions about what I'd seen the night before and selling lots of donuts almost as an afterthought, I glanced at the clock and saw that I had only another half hour before I was due to leave the donut shop in search of Gladys.

The only problem was that I still hadn't heard from Grace.

Where was she, and what was she doing that was so consuming that she couldn't return my call? I decided to try her number again.

It rang four times, and then it went straight to voicemail.

I was about to leave a message when my phone beeped, and I saw that Grace was trying to call me back.

"Hello?" I asked.

"Sorry I didn't get back to you sooner. I was following one of my reps around in a hotel, so I had my phone on mute so she wouldn't know that I was tailing her."

"What on earth were you following her around for?" I asked.

"I've had a few complaints about her absences over the last several days, and I wanted to see for myself why she was missing her appointments."

"What was she doing, carrying on a secret affair during working hours?" I asked.

"That I could have excused. No, she was interviewing with two of our competitors looking for a new job."

"Wow, how fast did you fire her?" I asked, knowing Grace wouldn't put up with something like that. Apparently I was wrong.

"Are you kidding? I offered her a ten percent bump in pay on the spot and another three days' vacation not to leave. She's too good to just let go."

"So you bribed her to stay?" I asked incredulously.

"Isn't that what salary and benefits are for?" she asked me. "Anyway, I got your message, and I'm in. I'll be there before you leave the shop."

"In half an hour?" I asked.

"You can count on it," she said.

After she hung up, I felt better about Grace going with me. I didn't believe for one second that Gladys might suddenly turn on me, but if she did, I wanted my best friend there beside me. If the unthinkable actually did happen, I doubted that the older cook could take both of us, at least not in such a public place.

I was still trying to figure out how best to approach Gladys when we started getting busy all of a sudden. Sometimes there was no rhyme or reason as to why business ebbed and flowed at the donut shop, but I'd learned not to question it, and to just enjoy any attention Donut Hearts was getting.

When the rush was over, it was nearly time for me to leave, and there was still no sign of Grace. I walked back into the kitchen and found Emma finishing up with the next-to-last round of dishes. "You don't have to stay late to do the final washing," I said. "I'll do it when I get in tomorrow morning."

"That's okay. I don't mind," she said with a grin. "Besides, your two days off start tomorrow, or had you forgotten?"

It had actually slipped my mind in the frenzy of what had been happening lately. "I can come in and work tomorrow, if you'd like."

"No, Mom and I will be fine. Are you going to meet up with Jake in Raleigh?"

Was it bad that I hadn't even considered doing that? "No, he needs some time alone with his sister and her kids."

"What are you going to do with yourself if he's gone?" Emma asked as she drained the sink and dried off her hands.

"Young lady, I was perfectly capable of filling my days before Jake Bishop ever came into my life," I said with a grin as I picked up a hand towel and swatted her gently with it.

"Sure you did," Emma said with a smile of her own. "You also used to work seven days a week, remember? I'm as big an advocate for Woman Power as the next gal, but it can be nice having someone else in your life."

"Sorry you're going through a rough patch in the dating department," I said. Emma had a tendency to fall in and out of love fairly easily. Were her standards too high? It wasn't for me to say, even though I suspected that it was true.

"It's fine. I've decided to dedicate the extra time I've got at the moment to become a better me," she said proudly.

"A worthwhile goal if ever there was one, not that you need it," I added quickly. "If you need me, call, okay? I won't be very far."

"I'll be fine," she said, and I knew that it was true.

We walked back out front together, and as I headed for the door, I said, "Thanks again for covering for me. I appreciate it."

"Not only am I happy to do it, that's what you pay me for,

remember?" she asked with a laugh. I was about to put my jacket on as I stepped outside, but I realized the day had warmed up quite a bit, so I put it over one arm and headed across Springs Drive to the park.

Gladys was easy to spot, and as I started in her direction, I heard a familiar voice from behind me call out, "Hey, wait for me."

Grace had made it after all.

"I wasn't sure you were going to get here in time," I said as she joined me.

"Suzanne, you should know by now that you should never doubt me," Grace said with a grin. "I even had time to go home and change first."

She was indeed wearing casual clothing, at least for her. Grace's blouse and slacks looked natural on her, but for me, it would be something I'd wear to a wedding, or maybe a job interview. The few times I got dressed up beyond jeans and a T-shirt, or maybe a sweater too, people always overreacted, as though I never wore nice things. I was just more comfortable in casual clothes, and I didn't mean Grace's definition. It was a good thing Jake loved me best dressed as I was right now; I was certain that it was one of the reasons I'd fallen in love with him. "You look wonderful, as usual," I told her.

She studied my outfit and frowned for a moment. "I'm envious of you. You know that, don't you?"

Her comment startled me. "Why is that?"

"You make that outfit look like a million dollars. If I tried to pull it off, I'd look like a hillbilly hobo. I have to dress this nice to get people to take me seriously. I'd kill to be able to do what you do so effortlessly."

I grinned at her before I spoke. "I was just thinking the

same thing about you and your style. We're a pair of odd birds, aren't we?"

She locked her arm in mine as we started to walk together. "I like us just fine the way we are." As we headed toward Gladys, Grace asked, "Do we have a game plan, or are we just going to wing it? I don't mind either way, but I thought I'd at least ask."

"I've been giving it a lot of thought all morning, and I've come to the conclusion that we should just come out and ask her about Gray point-blank," I admitted. "It's not going to do us much good beating around the bush, and we have less than half an hour before Gladys has to be at work. I'm not sure how Trish is going to feel about us grilling one of her cooks as it is."

"I'm sure that she'll understand," Grace said.

"I'm not so certain. She's pretty possessive about her people."

"We're not going to beat her up, Suzanne, we're just going to have a nice little chat."

"Let's just make sure we keep it friendly," I said. "We can both get a little intense sometimes, so we can't forget that these people are talking to us of their own free will. We don't have any way of compelling them to speak with us."

"You don't have to worry about me. I'll play nice," Grace said with a quick grin.

Gladys was sitting at a bench in the park near the gazebo, staring off into space. She didn't even realize that we had approached her until I spoke. "Mind if we join you for a minute or two?" I asked her.

The cook looked up with a start. "What? Oh, hello, girls. Certainly, why not?"

Grace sat on one side of her, and I took the other. The bench was crowded with all three of us, but we scrunched together to make it work. "First of all, we're both sorry for your loss," I said, starting right in. I'd meant what I'd told Grace; there was no time for small talk.

"You knew about me and Gray," she said as a statement of fact, an air of resignation in her voice. "I'm not surprised, though we did our best to keep our relationship secret. How is that you two always seem to know what's going on in April Springs?"

"You'd be amazed by just how much we miss every day," I said. Was that the reputation Grace and I had? Were we thought of as a pair of busybodies? Sure, we'd dug into a few murders in the past, and to do that, we'd had to ask a great many people some very uncomfortable questions, but I didn't think that was what defined us. I was the town donutmaker, Dot's daughter, Jake's wife, Emma's boss, Grace, Trish, and Emily Hargraves's friend, Max's ex-wife, and at least a dozen other things I could think of off the top of my head. Amateur sleuth was just one of the many labels that defined me, or at least I hoped so.

"And yet you are here," she said wearily.

"We really are sorry about Gray," Grace said, patting her shoulder. "It's tough to lose someone you care about. We can both testify to that fact."

Gladys nodded. My friend had found the perfect chord to strike with the woman. "I couldn't stay with him, not after what he told me, but I'm sorry for the way I broke his heart, and I'm in complete despair knowing that I'll never get another chance with him," Gladys said after a moment's pause.

"Did he tell you his secret?" I asked her, wondering if him stealing someone else's identity had been a deal-breaker for her.

Gladys turned abruptly to me. "How do you know anything about his past? Who told you, Suzanne? No one was supposed to know about that but me."

"I can't tell you how I know, just that I do," I said. I'd been talking about his false name and documentation, but Gladys was clearly talking about something much bigger than that. Now, if only we could get her to share it with us, we might have someplace to start digging.

"He lied to me the entire time we were together!" Gladys said with vehemence. "Gray wasn't who I thought he was. That wasn't even his name, but you clearly already know that! How could I trust him after he confessed the truth to me?"

"Was it really all that bad?" I asked, sincerely curious about how a man could keep a secret for twenty years and then suddenly let it just slip away. It didn't make sense, unless he'd done it intentionally, *wanting* Gladys to find out. How wearying it must have been to keep his secrets to himself all those years, and how lonely he must have felt being the only person who knew the truth.

"He only told me because he thought that someone from his past had come back to haunt him," she said. "It was killing him, so late one night, he started to confess it all to me."

"What did he say?" I asked, relieved that we were finally going to find out the truth.

"His real name wasn't Gray. It was Gary. He stole his name from a dead man because it was so close to matching his own. Who does that, Suzanne? It's a travesty to pass yourself off as someone else."

"Did he happen to mention his real last name?" I asked.

"Or more importantly, why he'd done it?" Grace followed up. She was right. That was a much more important question.

"Just that he'd been forced into taking such drastic steps to save himself. He told me that he'd gotten involved in something really bad. He knew that he was in over his head almost from the start, but when he tried to get out of it, one of the members of the group told him that he'd kill him if he tried to change his mind and back out. Gray—or Gary, I guess—said that he had no choice. I'm going to keep calling him Gray, since that's the only name I ever knew him by. Anyway, Gray didn't think anyone would get hurt, but things went wrong at the end, and someone died as they were getting away."

"From what, though, exactly?" Grace persisted.

"I don't know!" Gladys sounded distraught. "I'm guessing they stole something valuable, like money or gold, but I didn't give him a chance to explain. I told him that I never wanted to see him again, and then I ran out of his cabin. He kept trying to win me back, but I was too foolish to listen to him, and now I'll never get the chance."

"Would you have taken him back if he were still alive?" I asked softly, interested in her answer, not for the investigation, but for my own sake.

"I don't know," she said wistfully. "I don't suppose I'll ever know the answer to that question. He came to Movie Night for one last try with me. I knew that it was a big concession on his part. Gray hated being seen in public, especially lately. I have to admit that him coming meant a lot to me. I may have softened, but with a murder charge hanging over him from his past, I might not have had any choice. I urged him to give himself up and face the consequences for his actions, but he told me if he did that, he might as well take a gun to his head and end it all right then and there. He was a troubled man. I might not have known his real name, but I'd like to think that I knew the man he was, you know? Gray was good, and kind, and I can't imagine the circumstances that would force him into ending someone else's life."

That explained, at least to a certain degree, his past, but what about his present? "Was there anyone in town in particular that he'd been having trouble with lately?" I asked her. I noticed some movement behind the gazebo, but I couldn't tell if whoever was there was trying to listen in on our conversation, or if it was just a random person enjoying the park and the nice weather we were having.

"Yes, as a matter of fact, there was," she said with a frown.

"You don't honestly think someone from April Springs killed him, do you?"

"That's what we're trying to find out," I told her. "Don't worry about telling tales out of school. What you tell us will be strictly confidential."

"I'm not sure either one of you can promise me that," she said with a frown. "You're married to a former cop, and Grace is dating the chief of police right now."

"You can trust us," Grace said, and I nodded as well. It was an easier promise for me to keep since Jake was in Raleigh, but I knew if Grace gave her word, she'd stick to it, regardless of the consequences. "We won't tell anyone whatever you choose to share with us."

"In the end, I suppose that I'll have to trust you, because if either one of you betray me, you're going to have to deal with the wrath of my boss." She didn't smile as she said it, not that it would have done any good. She was right. I knew that if we broke our word to Gladys, we would lose more than a great place to eat; we'd lose one of our best friends as well. "Very well. It can't hurt Gray any more than he's already suffered. Let's start with Barry Vance."

"Why did Gray have trouble with the mailman?" I asked. Barry was big on snooping, and heaven help anyone who got a postcard and wanted to keep the contents confidential. I'd always thought of Barry as kind of harmless, but maybe I'd been wrong.

"I thought the same thing, but we were in Union Square eating at Napoli's when we ran into Barry a week ago. I swear, Gray turned white when Barry approached us. The mailman seemed awfully cocky about something, as though he knew something that he shouldn't have."

"Could he have found out about Gray's real identity?" I asked.

"I have no idea. All I know is that Gray was jumpy for the

rest of the night. He barely touched his food, and he loved Napoli's. He dropped me off at home right after we ate, and he couldn't get back home fast enough. We broke up right after that. Anyway, I thought it was odd, but after what happened to Gray, I think someone should talk to Barry. He knows more than he's willing to let on."

"That's helpful," I said. "Is there anyone else you can think of?"

"Donald Rand," she said flatly. I knew the investment broker from an earlier investigation. Grace and I had pretended to be people we weren't to get him to cooperate, but that wouldn't work anymore, since Rand had been by the donut shop half a dozen times since finding out who I really was. I wouldn't have trusted the man with my spare change, but had Gray? If the hermit had really stolen any money, would he bury it in his backyard, or would he invest it to try to wash it through Rand?

"Did he have any investments with the broker?" Grace asked.

"I believe so, but he never came right out and said it. All I can say for sure is that Gray was extremely upset with the man over the course of the past two weeks."

"Okay, we'll speak with him, too," I said.

"But you're not going to tell him that I told you about his connection with Gray, right?" Gladys asked, looking worried for a moment.

"Are you afraid of him, Gladys?" Grace asked her.

"You're kidding, right? Grace, at the moment, I'm afraid of everyone, including the two of you! Someone tied Gray to a tree and then stabbed him in the chest! I personally think you two are crazy going after someone who could do that. If the killer didn't find what they were looking for when they came after Gray, how long is it going to take them to come looking for me? I have half a mind to leave town until this all blows over, but I can't right now! The Food Bank needs me, and I won't let a killer run me off." She seemed to find a new level of resolve as she said it. "It's nearly time for me to go to work," she said. "I've told you all that I can. Find whoever did this to Gray, ladies. He might not have deserved a free pass after what he did, but he deserved better than he got."

As she got up from the bench, I noticed the person hiding behind the gazebo shift again. It was the stranger who'd asked about Gray before he was murdered!

I thanked Gladys, and then, to everyone's surprise, I sprinted straight for the gazebo.

The cook looked at me oddly, but I didn't even have to clue Grace in on what I was doing. Without a word, she ran with me.

I motioned for her to go one way, and I took the other.

But he was too quick for us.

He was already gone.

How much had he heard, and why was he so intent on eavesdropping on our conversation? I didn't know, but I was determined to find out.

CHAPTER 9

"**T**HIS IS CRAZY! HE COULDN'T have just vanished into thin air! Where did he go?" I asked Grace as we met at the back of the gazebo.

"Look. Someone's trying to sneak around the back of your cottage!" Grace said as she pointed to the retreating figure nearly hidden by the trees.

"You swing around by your house and come up the road," I shouted instructions as I chased after him. "I'll keep him from backtracking."

"What am I supposed to do if I catch him?" Grace asked as she began to do as I'd asked.

"Find a way to keep him there until I can get to you both," I said as I hurried away.

"Looking for something in particular?" I asked the man, nearly out of breath, as I found him lurking behind my cottage.

"I was thinking about buying the place," he said, doing his best to act nonchalant under my glaring scrutiny.

"Oh, really. I didn't realize that it was for sale."

"It's one of those private showing things," he said.

"Ordinarily I might be tempted to believe you, but I know for a fact that you're lying to me."

He slumped a little. "You know who really owns this place, don't you?"

"I do. It's mine. Bad luck. Why were you snooping on our conversation, and why did you run away when I spotted you? You're a smooth guy. Why didn't you just try to lie your way out of it?"

He grinned at me, an odd thing to see. "Believe it or not, I panicked. Whether you put any credence in it or not, I want to know what happened to Gray Vincent every bit as much as you do."

"I find that hard to believe," I said as Grace rushed up to join us. She looked at me quizzically, but I shook my head. I had this under control.

"It really doesn't matter what you believe," he said. "I've done nothing illegal here."

"Besides trespassing, you mean," I said. It was an interesting choice of words for him to use. Why would he go straight to illegal? Did that mean that this man had a past history as a criminal, just the same as Gray had? Were they in on something together in the past? Perhaps the robbery gone wrong that had cost someone his life? "You wouldn't mind showing me some identification, would you?"

That made him chuckle. "Why in the world should I do that?"

"If you have nothing to hide, why wouldn't you?"

"Because I hate busybodies like you and your friend, there," he said. His apparent good nature had melted away when I'd asked him for ID.

"Grace, call Chief Grant."

She pulled out her cellphone, and as she did, Wright started toward me. Was he going to try to attack me? I braced myself, but he walked right past me and headed back to the park.

"Where do you think you're going?" I asked him.

"Anywhere that's away from you and your friend."

As I started to follow him, I told Grace, "Tell Stephen we need him right now."

That got his attention. He stopped and turned toward me, and there was an ugly look on his face that gave me chills. "I'm only going to say this one time. Butt out of this, donut lady. You're in over your head."

"I often am, but that isn't going to keep me from finding out what really happened to my friend," I said, standing my ground.

"Suit yourself, but you've been warned."

He kept going, and I started to follow him again when Grace grabbed my arm.

I tried to free myself, but she wouldn't let go. "What are you doing?"

"Saving you from yourself, probably," she said. "Suzanne, that was an honest-to-goodness threat. Let Stephen handle it."

"Where is he, by the way?" I asked as I calmed down a little. When I was pushed, I tended to push back, but Grace was right. It was time to let a professional deal with this man. Unless I missed my guess, he'd seen plenty of trouble in his life, and had no doubt caused as much himself.

"There's a wreck outside of town. He's got his hands full at the moment, but he'll be here as soon as he can."

I looked back for the stranger who'd threatened me, but he was already gone.

Sooner or later we'd have to find a way to deal with him, but at the moment, Gladys had given us a few other folks to speak with. I wasn't about to be driven off this case, or any other. If I gave in to bullies, I might as well stop investigating on my own, and this was too important for me to walk away from.

"What should we do in the meantime?" Grace asked me.

"We need to speak with Barry Vance and Donald Rand," I said. "Any preferences as to which one we tackle first?"

"That's a little like asking me if I'd like to get punched in the face or kicked in the ribs, isn't it?" she asked me with a bit of a frown.

"Unfortunately, this time both of the suspects we know

aren't very nice people," I said. "If you don't have a preference, let's go see Donald first."

"Why the investor instead of the mailman?" Grace asked as we walked to my Jeep and got in.

"It's simple, really. At least we know where he usually is this time of day. Barry could be anywhere, but chances are good that we'll find Donald Rand in his cheesy little office in the strip mall."

"Then let's go," she said.

But our plans changed abruptly, as they had a way of doing sometimes. We were just reaching the heart of town when I saw the mailman walking his route, and I quickly pulled the Jeep over so we could speak with him first after all. Grace had been on her phone texting someone about something, and she looked up with alarm as I changed direction and movement so suddenly. "What's going on, Suzanne?"

"There's Barry," I said. "Do you want to come with me, or should I handle him alone? He might be more willing to talk if there's just one of us."

"I suppose it's worth a shot, but if you don't feel like tackling him alone, give me three minutes to finish with this. I'll be glad to join you," she said as she frowned. "I'm just trying to put out a fire at work so I can keep helping you."

"You do that, I'll handle this," I said.

"Are you sure?"

"No worries. If I get in trouble, I'll just scream," I said with a grin. "Besides, what's he going to do to me? This is about as public as it gets in April Springs." We were near the clock, and right across the street from city hall. It would be a stupid place to attack me, even if Barry felt the impulse.

"Promise?" she asked.

"I promise."

"Okay. Should I join you when I'm finished with this?"

"No, just wait here. I shouldn't be long."

I walked over to Barry, who was listening to something on his iPod as he walked his route. I doubted that was completely kosher, but what did I care? I wasn't there to enforce the US Postal Service's rules and regulations. I was looking for a murderer.

"Barry. Barry. Barry!" I finally shouted, trying to get his attention. The last time did it, and he stopped dead in his tracks as he pulled out his earbuds. He was an odd shape of a man, with a decent-sized belly but possessing the legs of a much younger man, no doubt from all of the walking he did on his job. Though there was still a chill in the air, especially in the mornings, he wore uniform shorts, as if to put his best foot forward, so to speak. His face looked a bit like a bird's, with a beaklike nose, long, narrow eyes, and a pointed chin.

"What is it, Suzanne? I haven't gotten to the donut shop yet, and I can't just dig through my bag looking for something special for you. I've got a schedule, and I'm sticking to it."

Barry wasn't a great mailman. Though my mailbox hung on the outside wall of the former train depot where I sold my treats, he'd refuse to walk in, even if he had something for me too big to fit into the box. Instead, he'd prop it up against the outside wall, as though he couldn't be bothered walking it the extra four steps inside to hand-deliver it to me. I couldn't remember the last time he'd actually stepped foot into Donut Hearts, business or personal, and we didn't exactly have a cordial relationship. "It's not about the mail. I need to talk to you about Gray Vincent."

That caught him off guard. "What about him? He wasn't on my route, so I barely knew the man. It's a shame what happened to him, but I can't help you."

I was on his daily route, and he didn't know me at all, either. Was he being a little too defensive? "That's not what I heard."

His eyes sharpened a little, and his mouth narrowed. "What are you talking about?"

"That there was bad blood going on between you two," I said.

"That's a lie," he said loudly and forcefully. "I know where you heard it. Gladys said something, didn't she?"

"What could she possibly say, if nothing happened between the two of you?" I asked him innocently.

"Nothing. If she, or anybody else, said anything happened between Gray and me, it was strictly in their imagination. Now I have to get back to work. Some of us put in a full day and don't cut out before lunchtime."

That was patently unfair, since I started my day before any sane person even thought about getting out of bed, but I decided to let it slide. It felt as though he was purposely goading me, trying to start a fight so he could end the conversation.

I wasn't going to let that happen. "We're going to find out what really was going on between the two of you," I said earnestly.

"Who's this 'we'?" he asked me, looking around. "Is your husband prying into other people's lives with you nowadays?"

"You never know," I said, hoping that Grace would do as I asked and stay in the Jeep. It was a lot more intimidating having a former state police investigator on your heels than it was a cosmetics company sales supervisor, though if he really knew Grace, I doubted that he'd feel that way.

"Fine. So something happened," Barry said. "He owed me a little money, but we cleared it up. That's it."

"Why would Gray owe you money?" I asked, curious about this sudden confession.

"It was from a poker game," the mailman said just a little too quickly. I couldn't imagine a more outrageous lie. Poker was, by its very nature, a social event, and Gray Vincent would barely leave his cabin, let alone be out among other people playing poker, or any other game.

"That should be easy enough to prove, then. Who else played that night?" I asked him, doing my best to present a face that didn't shout LIAR at him.

"It was a private game," he said quickly. "I wouldn't feel right mentioning any other names without their permission."

No doubt he was hoping that I'd just drop it. It was clear that Barry didn't know me at all. "That's okay. I'll ask around," I said.

As I started to walk away, Barry said, "I wouldn't do that if I were you."

"Why on earth shouldn't I?"

"Important people, powerful people, were playing. They won't like you snooping around, Suzanne."

I laughed. "In April Springs, I'm either friends with or related to every important or powerful person in town, and I know for a fact that Gray Vincent wouldn't come into town for anything short of a hurricane or a nuclear explosion."

I was four steps away when Barry stopped me. "Fine. It wasn't poker."

Wow. It hadn't taken him very long to give up that particular lie. As I turned back to him, I said, "I didn't think it was. So, if it wasn't poker, then what was it?"

"It was personal," Barry said guardedly. "If I wanted you to know, I'd tell you."

"Okay, but you should know that I'm not going to just let this go. I'm going to find out what really happened between you."

"Do whatever you want to," he said with a frown. "I've got to get back to my route." With that, he jammed the earbuds back in and tried his best to ignore me as he walked away.

Grace was just finishing up with her phone when I got back to the Jeep. "Catastrophe averted?" I asked her as I started it and continued on to Rand's office.

"For the moment," she said. "What did Barry have to say for himself?"

"He tried telling me that Gray owed him money because of a poker game, but he folded pretty quickly when I told him I didn't believe him."

"Did he tell you the truth then?"

"No, but it's obvious that Gladys saw something pass between them. I'm afraid that we're going to have to dig a little harder into the mailman's life to find out."

"We can do that," she said. "After all, that's one of the things we're best at."

"Let's forget about him for now and focus on Donald Rand. It's too bad we can't use a cover story with him, but after he found out that we lied to him once, he'd never believe another one."

"It was fun pretending to be someone else, wasn't it?" Grace asked me.

"I have to admit, once I got into the spirit of it, it could be," I agreed. "Unfortunately, this time we're going to have to just play this straight up."

CHAPTER 10

I T HAD BEEN YEARS SINCE I'd set foot in BR Investments, but nothing had changed as far as I could tell. The lone desk was the same cheap one I'd seen before, and the carpet was just as ugly a green, though perhaps a little more worn. Donald Rand was a little worse for the wear himself. His clothes were even more frayed than they'd been before, and his massive belly made me fearful that a button might pop off his shirt and blind me at any moment. At least he'd finally given up on nurturing the wispy strands of hair that had been precariously arranged on top of his head; he was now completely bald.

"Unless one of you ladies has suddenly come into a fortune you need help investing, I'm busy at the moment," he said the moment Grace and I walked into his office.

I saw Grace's face light up, and knew that if I didn't act quickly, one of us would be about to inherit a sizable fortune from some fictitious long-lost relative. "We're here about Gray Vincent's murder," I said.

Grace frowned at me for a moment for killing her fun, but we didn't have time to mess around.

"I don't talk about my clients with other people," he said flatly.

I glanced down at some of the paperwork spread out across his desk and caught a few glimpses of Gray's name written here and there.

Grace asked, "Should you even be admitting that he was a client of yours, if that's the case?"

Rand frowned, realizing that she was probably right. "I don't know anything about Gray's murder," he said dully. "So don't bother asking."

"You two didn't get along very well, did you?" I asked him. "I'm really surprised he kept you on as his financial advisor."

Rand's face darkened. "We got along just fine."

"Really?" I asked, leaving it up to him to fill the silence that only grew between us. It was an old trick that Grace and I liked to use when the situation called for it. It was amazing how many people would do their best to fill in empty gaps in conversation, if you just gave them enough opportunity to talk and fill the voids.

He couldn't take it for very long. "I don't care what you heard. I advised him on something, and he did just the opposite. When I pressed him on it, he pushed back. I was right, I knew that he was making a mistake. How could I not try to talk him out of it? Was he happy with me? Probably not, but he would have come around sooner or later."

I caught Grace's glance, motioned to the desktop, and then pled for her to make a distraction for me.

I wanted a better look at that paperwork.

My partner caught on immediately. She started to put her purse down on the edge of the desk and then "accidentally" spilled the contents onto the carpet. "I can't believe I'm so clumsy," she said loudly. I thought she was overacting, as she had a tendency of doing sometimes, but evidently Rand didn't have a problem with it. Both of them dropped to their knees to recover the contents while I did a quick scan of the desktop. Grace did her part; she'd reach to pick something up, only to knock it farther away. Rand grew tired of the game quickly, though, and that's when he must have noticed what I was really doing.

He stood up quickly and covered his desktop with his jacket. "See anything interesting, Suzanne?" he asked me sarcastically.

I decided to tell the truth. "Why was Gray Vincent in the process of changing his beneficiary?"

"Get out of my office," Rand said slowly.

"But my purse," Grace protested, trying in vain to buy us a little more time.

"I'll mail anything else I find to you," he snapped. "You are both trespassing. Now leave!" The last bit was said with a great deal of force.

We had no choice. Grace scooped up the last bits of the contents of her purse, and we did as we were told.

Once we were outside, Grace asked me, "Suzanne, what exactly did you see in there? I thought he was going to take a run at us both on the spot."

"It was paperwork for a brokerage account Gray evidently had with Rand. I saw a change of beneficiary form letter on top. There weren't many blank spaces, and two of them were already filled in."

As we walked back to the Jeep, she asked, "Whose names did you see?"

"I couldn't tell which was which, but I know for a fact one was Rand's name, and another was Gladys. It appeared to me that Gray was about to change his beneficiary. If he was going to take Rand's name off the forms and replace them with Gladys's, it could give the broker a motive for murder. He knew that he had to strike before the paperwork was officially filed so he could get control of the account."

"What if he was changing the forms from Gladys to his name instead?" Grace asked me.

"Why would he do that?" I asked.

"They broke up, remember? If their relationship really was over in Gray's mind, why wouldn't he give his money to someone else? Why not his investment counselor? If that was the case, how would Gladys react if she knew that she was going to lose her inheritance from Gray? For all we know, she was counting on the cash."

"Are you saying that you think she killed him for his money?" I asked her. The idea was difficult to wrap my mind around. I never would have thought of the older cook as a gold digger, but it was clear that events may have been interpreted exactly that way.

"Suzanne, we've both seen murder committed for money in the past. Just because we think we know Gladys doesn't mean that she might not be capable of it herself."

"I know you're right, but still I'm having a hard time believing it," I said after a few moments.

"We need to dig into Gladys's life a little more than we thought we might have to," Grace said. "Maybe there's a pressing reason that she needs money, like a dying sister or something."

"I still don't think she'd kill someone," I said.

"I don't want to either, but if we're going to do this, we need to be thorough. Just because we like her, we can't just forget about her involvement in this case."

"Agreed," I said.

I didn't like it, but what choice did I really have? As I drove back toward the donut shop, I was surprised to see Gabby Williams standing out in front of her shop.

The moment she saw my Jeep, she started waving in my direction.

"What do you suppose she wants?" Grace asked me as I pulled my vehicle into a parking spot in front of Gabby's shop.

"I don't know, but I have a hunch we're about to find out."

"Who was that man you two were chasing around in the park earlier?" Gabby asked the moment we were all inside her store.

Before I answered, I looked around the shop to make sure that it was empty. There were no customers, but I found some really nice items, gently used clothing pieces that were more fit for Grace than they ever would be for me, and a mannequin that appeared to be looking at my outfit with disdain. Why shouldn't it? It was dressed much more nicely than I was.

"You saw that, did you?" I asked her.

"How could I miss it? Once moment you were talking with Gladys while the three of you were sitting on a bench in the park, and the next thing I know, you both take off running as though the pair of you were on fire. I'd seen that strange man hovering around town earlier, but I didn't realize that he had anything to do with Gray's murder."

"We don't know that he does one way or the other just yet," I said, trying to keep our conversation as cryptic as I could manage.

"Then why on earth did you chase him?"

It was a fair question. "I thought he might be eavesdropping on our conversation," I said. "When I went over to see what he was up to, he was gone."

"But you found him soon enough, didn't you?"

I raised an eyebrow. "Gabby, how can you possibly know that? I understand that you can see the gazebo from your window, but I know for a fact that you can't see my cottage." I glanced through the window to be sure that I was right. Sure enough, the trees blocked the view.

"I was concerned for your safety, both of you," she amended quickly. "Naturally I wanted to be sure that you two were okay. I went as far into the park as I needed to in order to confirm that you were both okay, and then I came straight back to the shop."

"The truth is, we need more information about him," I conceded. "But what could we do? He decided to leave, and there wasn't anything we could do to stop him."

"I'll keep an eye out for him in the future," she promised,

which I knew might be of some help. There was little that Gabby missed in our little town. She added, "A little later, I saw you talking to Barry Vance, Suzanne," she said. "I must say, I'm not surprised you think he might be up to something."

"Do you honestly suspect him of killing Gray?" I asked her.

"Does it matter what I think?" she asked. "*You* were the one grilling him on Springs Drive. By the way, it was brave of you to face him alone. Where were you, Grace?"

"I was in the Jeep taking care of some business," she said firmly, "but if Suzanne had needed me, I was just ten steps away."

"And I wasn't grilling him," I corrected her. "We were just having a conversation about his relationship with Gray. You should know from firsthand experience that's the main way we've been able to figure *anything* out in the past. Grace and I are just gathering information at this point," I said. "Is there some reason in particular we should have him on our radar?" Even though Gabby had given us Gladys's name as a lead, I wasn't about to disclose the fact that the cook had told us to speak with Barry. I'd promised to respect the cook's wishes, and that was exactly what I was going to do.

"No, but it wouldn't surprise me one bit," Gabby said. "He almost lost his job last year. Did you know about that?"

"What happened?" Grace asked. She was still tentative about dealing with Gabby, as the two hadn't always gotten along well in the past. I knew one thing with full certainty; Gabby Williams was a bad enemy to have, and I was glad that she and my best friend had come to some sort of understanding. They might not be the best of buddies, but at least they'd found grounds for mutual respect, if not affection.

"He's a snoop," she said in explanation.

"So are we, for that matter," I said without thinking. "What else can you call what we do?"

Gabby raised one eyebrow. "Are you talking about you and Grace, or the two of us?"

"Us, not you," I quickly corrected her. Gabby was indeed nosier than Grace and me put together, but it wouldn't do any of us any good calling her on it.

She seemed mollified by my answer. "Don't be too hard on yourselves. He's on a level you can't even imagine."

"What does he do, read other people's postcards before he delivers them?" Grace asked lightly.

"I'm really not at liberty to say," she said smugly. That was the Gabby Williams I knew. She may or may not have had something on the mailman, but if she could keep from disclosing the fact either way, I knew that she'd score it as a personal victory.

"Okay, so he's bad at his job. How does that tie in with Gray? Evidently there was *something* going on between them," Grace said. She wasn't exactly violating any confidences, but I wondered about the wisdom of sharing that information with Gabby.

"Did you ask him directly about it?" she wondered aloud. "Sometimes people will readily confess to the most unusual things if you only ask."

"We did. At first he said that Gray owed him money from a poker game."

"That's complete and utter nonsense," Gabby said quickly before I could finish.

"Which I told him. He immediately backed down from that lie, but when I pressed him more about it, he pretended to get offended and ended the conversation. He was clearly hiding something; I just don't know what."

"Keep digging," Gabby said. "You'll find it. Who else have you spoken with?"

I was about to deflect the question when Grace answered, "Donald Rand."

I gave her a sharp look, but she just shrugged in response.

Gabby pursed her lips in thought a moment before replying.

"That's interesting. It's hard to imagine Gray having enough money to invest with Rand. I know one thing; the man's bad at his job, and he takes a commission for his mistakes, to boot. Then again, Gray hasn't had any obvious means of support since he first came to town. He's been living on *something* all these years."

"I thought he retired," I said.

"Clearly he did, but from what, exactly? Did Rand have anything to share? You know he's in dire straights, don't you?"

I hadn't heard about that. "I'm not sure what you're talking about."

"I'm surprised you missed it," Gabby said, arching one eyebrow. "The rumor is that he's about to declare bankruptcy. As I said, he's bad at what he does, so that's not really that great a shock, but I also heard something much darker."

"What's that?"

"That he's been stealing from some of his clients," Gabby said in a near whisper, though the three of us were still all alone in the shop.

"Do you have any proof of that?" Grace asked her.

"No, but when there's enough smoke, there's bound to be a fire somewhere."

It was my turn to reveal something we'd uncovered. "I wonder if that might explain why he had some paperwork on his desk naming a new beneficiary for Gray's investments with him. What better time to steal from someone than after they're past caring?"

"Oh ho! That might be your motive right there."

"Actually, there were two names on the documents that I could see," I said, "but I couldn't determine who was getting his money, and who was going to be losing it."

"What were the names, Suzanne?"

Before Grace could tell her, I said, "I'd rather not say until I know more about it."

Gabby looked frustrated by my refusal. "Honestly, how do you expect me to help you if you won't share your information with me?"

"It's not that I don't trust you," which I didn't. "I just don't want you thinking badly about either party on my account in case I'm wrong," I said, mostly wanting to protect Gladys's good name.

"Especially since one of them was your friend," Grace let slip out.

"What friend are you referring to?" Gabby asked with ice in her voice.

Grace knew instantly that she'd finally revealed too much. "I shouldn't have said that. I'm sorry."

"It's got to be Gladys," Gabby said firmly. "Is she inheriting Gray's fortune, or is Rand trying to cheat her out of it?"

So, now it was a fortune, even though we didn't even know how much Gray had invested with Rand in the first place. "We don't know anything about which name was going to be named the new beneficiary with any level of certainty just yet," I said quickly. "Besides, from what I could see, the documents hadn't even been signed yet, so it's probably nothing. That's why we didn't want to say anything."

I was doing my best to be calm and reasonable, but that wasn't how Gabby wanted to play it. "Do you two honestly believe Gladys had something to do with what happened to Gray? I can say with utter certainty that she would never kill someone for money. It's ridiculous. That woman wouldn't hurt a fly."

"We're not saying that she would," I said. "But since you brought it up, how can you be so sure that she wouldn't? I honestly believe that, given the right circumstances, *anyone* can commit murder. Does Gladys need money desperately for anything that you know of, perhaps a sick relative, or maybe she was about to lose her house?"

One of my guesses appeared to strike a nerve. They had both been stabs in the dark, but one of them had paid off. "I don't care if Gladys was about to be evicted, or if her sister needed an operation! She would never do such a thing, and I'll ask you to leave my shop this very instant!"

Gabby Williams was angry, and she was making no attempt to disguise it. "We're trying to help, Gabby. We like Gladys," I said.

She wouldn't listen to another word.

As she walked us out the door, she said frostily, "Then you have a funny way of showing it. Good day."

Gabby didn't even hang around for a response as she slammed the door in our faces. I heard the deadbolts click into place, and the CLOSED sign suddenly appeared in the window, though it was nowhere near time for her to shut her business down for the day.

Grace looked horrified when I glanced in her direction. "I am so sorry. Suzanne, what did I just do?"

"Don't worry about it. She'll calm down eventually," I reassured her, though I wasn't about to put it to a timetable. Gabby could forgive a transgression overnight, or she could chew on it like a dog with a bone for years; only time would tell which this would be.

"I wanted her to like me, that's why I said so much," Grace said, nearly crying as she said it. "Why is pleasing that woman important to me?"

"Gabby's opinion carries a lot of weight in this town," I said.

"And now she hates me. I'm so sorry I said anything."

"Don't be," I said, doing my best to reassure her. "It wasn't without results. Did you see her flinch when I mentioned the possibility that Gladys might be desperate for money?"

"It was pretty clear when she got so defensive all of a sudden. Suzanne, should we be looking at Gladys as a more viable suspect than we have been?"

"I don't know how we can't, given the papers we just saw. Greed can be an awfully powerful motive for murder, and it can turn the nicest people into vicious killers if they're desperate enough."

"Trish is not going to be happy with us," Grace said after a moment's reflection.

"She's just going to have to get in line then, isn't she?" I asked.

"So, what do we do now?" Grace asked me.

I was about to answer when her cellphone rang. She glanced at, and then stepped away as she said, "I have to get this."

After a few moments of hushed conversation, she hung up and turned back to me. "That was Stephen."

"Did he ask you out to dinner, because if he didn't, I happen to be free tonight. I thought we might go to Napoli's, if you didn't have any plans."

"That sounds lovely, but I'm not sure we're going to be able to go anywhere."

"Why not?"

"He's got something to tell us, something big that's going to change the entire course of the investigation."

"And he's willing to share it with us?" I asked, surprised at the level of access we were getting to a formal police investigation.

"It can't be anything official. That's why he wants to meet us on my front porch. He's already there waiting for us right now."

"Then let's go," I said. We jumped into the Jeep and drove to Grace's, though we could have easily walked the short distance.

I had a reason for getting there so quickly.

I wanted to get there before the police chief had a chance to change his mind.

CHAPTER 11

"LADIES, THANKS FOR COMING," THE chief said as we approached Grace's front porch. He looked a lot older to me since he'd taken on the responsibilities of being the police chief full time from Jake. Was he losing weight? His uniform seemed a little baggy on him, and there were wrinkles around his eyes that I could swear hadn't been there before.

"We couldn't exactly turn you down, Chief," I said as I took one of the free chairs outside. Grace detoured toward him long enough to give him a quick peck on the lips.

"Before you say anything," she told him, "you need to be sure that you're comfortable sharing it with us."

"You're not trying to discourage him from helping us, are you?" I asked her with a grin. I'd fought my share of police chiefs in my time, even my own husband, so I wasn't sure that was the right way to deal with one who was doing so freely and willingly.

"You of all people should understand why I'm asking," she said. "Didn't Jake quit being the police chief directly because of some of the things we did in our investigations?"

"I'm not sure that's entirely fair," I said. "He was always going to be the temporary chief here. He wouldn't have handed the job over to the new chief if he hadn't been certain that he was ready."

"Hey, I'm sitting right here. You can both see me, right?" Chief Grant asked with a grin. He reached over and patted

Grace's hand. "I appreciate your concern, but I'm not violating any rules by sharing this information with you. It's going to be public knowledge soon enough anyway, so I don't see any harm in giving you both a head start."

"What's so earthshattering?" I asked him, no longer able to contain my curiosity.

"I found out who Gray really was, and more importantly, why he was hiding in April Springs."

"How bad is it? Gladys told us a little bit about his past earlier, but she didn't know many facts to back anything up," I said, feeling myself tense up inside. I realized that my image of an old friend was about to be changed forever, and I wasn't sure I wanted to hear it on one level, though I knew that if Grace and I were going to pursue our investigation, I'd need to know. Gladys had given us the general outline of what had driven him to April Springs twenty years earlier, but I wasn't sure I could handle the specific details.

"It's pretty bad, actually," he said solemnly.

"Did he kill someone?" Grace asked him.

"Not directly," the chief said. "It might be easier if I tell this my way. Do you mind?"

"Sorry," I said in quick apology. "Go on. I'll try not to interrupt you again."

He grinned at me. "I appreciate the offer, but I won't hold you to it. Gray Vincent's real name was Gary Manchester. He had a police record, with two convictions for breaking and entering, but there were no outstanding warrants for his arrest for the past twenty years. As far as the official law enforcement community was concerned, he'd served his time and was not wanted for any other crimes, not even a parking ticket."

"Then why hide his identity, as well as his past?" Grace asked. "I understand if he didn't want folks to know that he was a convicted felon, but it seems a little drastic doing all that he did to hide his past."

"That's not why he did it, at least according to one source I was able to uncover. It's all unofficial, but I believe it nonetheless. Just before Gray showed up in April Springs, there was a heist in upstate New York, and rumor had it that he was directly involved in it."

I'd promised not to comment until the chief was finished, but that clearly wasn't going to happen. "What did they steal? Gold? Cash? What?"

"He and two accomplices allegedly made off with two Monets, a Degas ballerina, and a Van Gogh haystack from a private collector, a man who'd amassed his fortune as a landscape architect," the chief told us.

"Was the collector killed during the crime?" Grace asked.

"Not directly, but his only living relative, a son unexpectedly visiting him at the time, was shot as the thieves escaped. In a way, the owner was killed at that moment too, because when he discovered the theft and saw his son dead on the floor, he had a heart attack and died instantly. It wasn't technically during the commission of the crime, but they might as well have put a gun to the man's heart and pulled the trigger."

"How awful," I said.

"The thieves were clever," the chief continued. "Instead of trying to sell the artwork on the open market, they negotiated with the insurance company for twenty-five percent of the artwork's overall value in exchange for its safe return."

"The insurance company actually negotiated with the thieves?" I asked incredulously.

"It happens more than you might imagine," Chief Grant said. "The amount they paid to get the artwork back was one and a half million dollars, deposited in an offshore bank account upon the safe return of the artwork."

"Half a million apiece was a pretty good haul back then," I said. "But that was twenty years ago. Why would someone kill Gray for it now? Surely he didn't have anything like that when he died."

"No, he didn't, but he wasn't exactly broke, either," the chief said. "When I questioned Donald Rand earlier, he told me that Gray had just liquidated half his portfolio a few days before he died. He was planning on leaving town, and he didn't want Rand handling his money anymore. Rand convinced him to do it in two chunks instead of all at once. He said it had something to do with tax ramifications, but I had a feeling that he wasn't ready to give up control of all of it at once."

"What did he do with the money he received?" I asked.

The chief smiled. "That's an excellent question. Gray made two hundred thousand dollars from the first half of the liquidation, and he took it all directly in cash. Rand was fussing about having to carry around that much money, but it all fit into a briefcase, and that's how Gray walked out of the office with it. The problem is, the cash has disappeared, and no one knows what happened to it."

I whistled softly under my breath. "Two hundred thousand dollars in cash is certainly a motive for murder in some circles. Do you think someone local found out about the money and killed him for it?"

"It's possible, but I'm working off another possibility at the moment. One of his suspected partners in the crime died last week, but not before leaving some pretty incriminating clues behind."

"Do you think the third partner tracked Gray here to April Springs?" I asked.

"At this point it's all supposition, but it makes sense. Have either of you seen this man around town lately? He's currently going by the name of Mickey Wright. Supposedly, he was the one who shot the collector's son during the heist." The chief pulled out an old mug shot, and a more recent image to go along with it.

I barely had to glance at it. It was the same man who'd been asking me about Gray earlier, the man Grace and I had accosted at my cottage earlier. "He's here in town. I don't know what his name is, but he's been asking around about Gray."

"What? And you didn't think that was important enough to mention it to me?"

"We tried," I said, "but you've been tied up with that wreck, and then we sort of got sidetracked. We weren't keeping it from you."

The police chief was still frowning as he asked, "Where exactly did you see him last?"

"He was trying to eavesdrop on our conversation with Gladys Murphy in the park today," Grace told him.

"You didn't confront him, did you?" the chief asked softly. "Please tell me at least that much."

"I wish we could, but how were we supposed to know that he was a bad guy?" I asked. After I brought him up to date on our conversation at my cottage, I said, "In our defense, we called you right away, but you were dealing with your own problems. When he left the park, he wasn't too happy with either one of us."

"This is bad, isn't it?" Grace asked.

"Do you think?" the chief asked sarcastically. "He's a suspected killer, and you two have gone out of your way to antagonize him. In what world could that be considered good?"

"My question is if Wright killed Gray for his money, why is he still hanging around here?" I asked.

"What do you mean?" Grace asked.

"He clearly didn't get the cash, or he would have already taken off. Either Gray hid it and wouldn't divulge where it was, or someone else beat Mickey Wright to the punch."

"This man is a pro," the chief said. "I don't think he would kill Gray without getting the money first."

"Why do you say that?"

"Gray was stabbed only once, and there were no other signs that he'd been hurt before that happened. That tells me that either he gave the money up quickly in an effort to save his own life, or someone got a little too eager and killed him before they had their hands on the cash."

"So, it doesn't make sense that Mickey Wright would keep hanging around if he already got the money," I said.

"Not unless he thought there was more cash that he could get his hands on," the chief said.

"He couldn't get access to Gray's account with Rand, could he?" I asked.

"I don't see how, but that doesn't mean that he believed Gray if he told him the two hundred thousand was all that he had," the chief answered. "Either way, I've got a hunch that Mickey Wright is the key to this mess, and I plan on finding him and then sweating the truth out of him."

Grace frowned when he said that. "Be careful, Stephen. If you're right, he's already killed at least two people that we know of, and I doubt he's the kind of guy to let a cop stop him from looking for that money."

"Don't worry about me. I can handle myself," the chief said.

"I'm not saying that you can't, but you still need to treat him like some kind of venomous snake."

"He's worse than that," the chief said. "After all, the snake is just doing what it was meant to do. This guy *chose* to be a thief and a killer."

"So, where do we come in?" I asked him. As much as I appreciated him sharing information with us, I knew that there was a price we were going to be asked to pay. "You're not asking us to bow out now, are you?"

"No, I know better than that," he said with a wry smile. "Just concentrate on the folks who live around here and focus on the present; leave the past and Mr. Wright to me."

"We can do that," I said. I wasn't about to remind him that if someone in town had stolen two hundred thousand dollars, they might kill to keep it. I stood and said, "Thanks for sharing this with us."

"I'm glad we could have this little unofficial, informal chat," he said. "Just between the three of us, I'm going to lock this town down tight until I find Mickey Wright, but until I do, stick together, will you?"

"We will," I promised.

"Well, I've got to get back out there. May I make a suggestion before I go?"

I shrugged. "I don't see why not." That didn't mean that I was necessarily going to follow it, but I didn't see any reason to share that with him.

"Why don't you two have a slumber party tonight over here? Jake's out of town, and I'm going to be tied up most of the night. I'd sleep better if I knew that you two were together."

"Why not at the cottage?" I asked, and then I realized what his answer would be. "Strike that. Wright saw us there, and I admitted it was my place, so if he decides to come after either one of us, that's where he's going to look. It doesn't mean that he can't find Grace's house, though. After all, it's not that far down the street from me."

"Just indulge me this once, would you?" the chief asked.

"Fine. I'm game if you are," I told Grace. I'd stayed there a few times in the past, though we normally had our sleepovers at my place.

"It will be nice hosting you for a change," she said.

"Then it's settled," the chief said. "Suzanne, if you need

anything from your house, I'll drive you over there and go inside with you."

"Do you really think that's necessary?" I asked him. The chief was clearly spooked by what was going on. I was taking it all very seriously, but evidently not as much as he was.

"Just humor me, okay? Can you imagine what Jake would do to me if something happened to you on my watch?"

He was right. "Okay. I'll be quick about it." I turned to Grace. "Are you coming with us?"

"No, you two go on. I've got to get the guestroom ready, and then I need to make a few quick phone calls."

"I'm not inconveniencing you, am I?" I asked.

She hugged me in reply. "Are you kidding? I'm glad Stephen suggested it. I'll see you soon."

Though the chief offered me a ride in his squad car, I decided to take the Jeep for the short drive to my cottage. After all, if I was hiding out from the killer, it wouldn't do for him to spot my vehicle in front of Grace's place on the off chance that Chief Grant was right. Personally, I had a feeling that Wright was long gone, but it wasn't exactly going to be a hardship staying overnight with my best friend, so I went along with it. I grabbed a few things and stuffed them into an overnight bag, but only after the chief did a thorough inspection of the cottage. I was glad I hadn't allowed myself to be messy with Jake's absence.

"I'll take that ride now," I said as I headed for his car with him.

"That's smart thinking," the chief said.

"I get a good idea every now and then," I replied with a grin. I'd been a fan of the man's since he'd been a new cop on the force. He'd come by the donut shop enough for us to become friends over the years, and when he'd started dating Grace, we'd grown even closer. He was quite a bit younger than we were, but it was funny how that mattered less and less the older I got.

We rode the short distance back to Grace's, and as I got out, I said, "Thanks again."

"For the information, or the chauffeur service?"

"For both of those things, and for looking out for us, too," I said.

"My pleasure," he said.

I closed his door, and he drove away.

Swinging my bag, I walked up the steps and joined Grace inside.

CHAPTER 12

I found Grace in the kitchen. "You're not cooking, are you?" I asked her with a grin. My best friend was many things, but a gourmet chef wasn't among them.

"I thought I might whip something up for us," she said as she frowned, staring blankly into one of her nearly empty cupboards.

"We could always call out for a pizza," I suggested.

"We could, but is there any reason we shouldn't go to Napoli's?"

"The chief was pretty clear that he wanted us both here," I reminded her.

"I took that to mean later tonight. We've got loads of time until we go to sleep, and he didn't say a word about us not going out of town for a quick bite. What do you say?"

I liked the local pizza enough to get it every now and then, but it was no match for Angelica DeAngelis and her girls in Union Square. "I'm in, but you're going to have to drive, unless you want to walk up the street and get my Jeep."

"Let's take my car. I can drop off some samples in Union Square, so no one's going to have a problem with me driving my company vehicle."

"It's a deal," I said. "Are you going to at least call the chief and tell him what we're planning to do?"

She grinned impishly at me. "I'm way ahead of you. I already did."

"You kind of took my willingness to go to Napoli's for granted, didn't you?" I asked her with a smile of my own.

"Seriously, what are the odds that you would say no to that offer?"

"Somewhere between slim and none," I admitted. "Let's go."

As we drove, I asked her, "Can I ask you something? Do you think Mickey Wright could have killed Gray?"

"I don't," she said. "If he had disappeared right after the murder and the cash was missing, I would have put some serious money on it, but I can't see him killing Gray without getting the cash first, can you? And if he's not sticking around to look for the money, why else would he still be here?"

"I have no idea," I said, feeling sorry for my friend dying the way he had, despite what he might have done twenty years ago. "Maybe there's more to it than that. I know what the chief said, but is there a chance Mickey Wright killed Gray in a fit of rage, maybe for some past sin we don't know about?"

"Does Wright seem like that kind of guy to you?" Grace asked me.

"No, not really. He was pretty cold and calculating when we cornered him at the cottage," I answered.

"So then, we're going to keep working off the premise that it was most likely someone from his present and not his past."

"It seems that way to me. Barry could have done it, if the mailman found out about the cash."

"Who knows?" Grace asked. "Maybe he snooped into the wrong piece of mail and realized that Gray had a lot more money than he seemed to."

"It had to be more than that, though," I said. "It's frustrating only knowing *some* of what we need to know." I could see Barry possibly killing someone for the money, but only if he could justify it by knowing something the victim had done in his past.

"What about Donald Rand?" Grace asked me.

"If he was changing that beneficiary form to favor himself, I can see it happening with no problem whatsoever. He probably felt as though he'd already let half the money slip through his fingers, and let's not forget, he's the only person we know for sure who was aware of the fact that Gray had a great deal of cash on him all of a sudden."

"Let's look at it from the opposite angle. What if Gray told Gladys that she was going to get everything? After all, they were extremely close. She might not have known that Gray hadn't officially changed the paperwork yet."

"Can you seriously see that sweet old cook killing someone for cold, hard cash, Grace?"

"Suzanne, we've seen it before. Money can bring out the best in people, but it usually acts just the opposite. If she were desperate for cash, she might not have felt as though she had any choice."

"We need to talk to Trish," I said, hating myself for saying it even as the words left my lips.

"Do you really think she's going to help us hang someone on her staff? I know that Trish is like family to both of us, but the two women who cook for her are like substitute mothers. She's not going to throw either one of them under the bus, not even for us."

"Not knowingly," I said in agreement.

Grace risked a quick glance in my direction. "Seriously? You're going to take a chance of ruining our friendship with Trish over this?"

"I'm not saying we do anything over the top. Let's just have a conversation with her. What can that hurt?"

"I don't even want to think about it. Do you mean right

now? Before we even eat?" Grace asked, clearly unhappy about the immediate prospect of cornering our old friend.

"Not on empty stomachs," I said. "It can wait until after we eat."

"That's the spirit," Grace replied, clearly relieved about delaying the confrontation. "Who knows? Maybe while we're dining on fine Italian cuisine, something else will come up in the meantime."

"Do you really think it might?"

"No, but it's not too much to hope for," she said. "Besides, we'll be at Napoli's in ten minutes. All I want to focus on right now is my empty belly."

I wasn't sure we were going to be able to satisfy our hunger when we got there. The strip mall where the restaurant was located didn't have a single parking space available. As Grace circled around yet again searching for a free spot, she asked in dismay, "Do you think *everyone* is here for dinner?"

I shook my head as I pointed to a sign close to the restaurant. "Unless I miss my guess, *that's* the reason for the traffic jam." A shop two doors down from Napoli's was clearly where all of the people were. A banner out front proclaimed that the place was going out of business, and that prices had been slashed ruthlessly. It appeared to offer a variety of things, from dishware to towels to who knew what else. We lucked out when a woman in a Cadillac built sometime in the seventies pulled out and nearly clipped the bumper of the car across from it. Grace snaked her car into the spot, to the chagrin of two other drivers hovering nearby.

"I love winning," she said with a broad grin as we got out.

"Even a parking spot?"

"Even that. These days I'll take what I can get."

"Are we dropping those samples off on the way back home?" I asked her.

"Whoops. They're already closed. I'll have to come back another time." It was clear she'd known they would be all along. I just laughed. Grace never failed to make the system work for her whenever she could.

We walked in and found Maria standing idly by at the front door. "It's so nice to see friendly faces," she said as she showed us to a table. There were only a few other diners there, and the place had a somber quality to it that I hadn't seen before. "I'll go get Mom."

"You don't have to," I said, but it was to Maria's retreating back. Jake would have loved the view, as would most men with a pulse. And why wouldn't they? Angelica and her daughters were classically beautiful, with the mother outshining even her own daughters. Age, as well as multiple childbirths, had done nothing to dull her essence.

"Ladies, have you come to save me?" Angelica asked dramatically as she walked out of the kitchen.

"We didn't know that you needed saving," I said as I stood and hugged her. Angelica wrapped me up in her arms and then found room for Grace as well. As we retook our seats, I asked, "What's going on?"

"Belinda Jakes has decided to go out of business," Angelica said gravely.

"That's too bad," Grace answered.

"It would be, if she'd ever actually do it, but this nonsense has been going on for two months! Just this morning, we saw another truckload of wares being unloaded in back. I have a feeling this bankruptcy is going to continue as long as it's profitable. In the meantime, my customers can't find a parking space, and we're feeling the pinch. We may be forced to close our doors."

Was that possible? I didn't know what I'd do without Angelica and her daughters, not to mention the food! "Are things really that dire?"

"They aren't good," Angelica said. "Enough of my problems, though. Since we're slow anyway, I've been experimenting with new lasagna recipes. Would you two mind terribly being my guinea pigs? There won't be a charge, of course, I just ask for your honest opinions."

"We don't mind paying for the privilege," I said.

"I should be the one paying you," she answered with a grin. Four minutes later, Angelica hand-delivered a platter filled with different types of lasagna, from spinach to spicy meat to cheese to a few more exotic combinations. They were each carefully marked with little placards, and it was more food than Grace and I could eat in three days.

"It's too much," I said as I surveyed the riches in front of us.

"Nonsense. I just brought a taste of each. Now try them and tell me what you think. Honest opinions only; be brutal if you must."

I expected the restaurateur to go back into the kitchen, but to my surprise, she pulled out one of the empty chairs at our table and sat down to watch us sample her food.

I took my first bite, the lasagna made with multiple cheeses, and let the experience wash over me. The layers offered the perfect blend of goodness, the cheese complemented perfectly by the sauce and the pasta. "What is in this?" I asked incredulously.

Grace had been watching me, so she took a bite of her own. Her face lit up as well. "It's incredible."

Angelica looked pleased by the praise. "I used a little mascarpone, some ricotta, a bit of provolone, a taste of mozzarella, and some parmesan. Then I use a few other small bits that I'm keeping to myself. Do you like it?"

"It's the most amazing thing I've ever tasted in my life," I said quite honestly.

Angelica just grinned as Grace nodded in agreement.

"Oh, wait until you taste what's next."

Grace and I left an hour later, both of us nearly too full to make the trip safely back to April Springs. "I'm not sure I can stay awake," I said. "I'm stuffed."

"At least you don't have to drive," Grace groaned. "I just want to go home and crawl into bed. You're on your own tonight."

"We still need to talk to Trish, remember?" I asked. I didn't relish having the conversation either, but what could we do? A murderer was on the loose in our quaint little town, and we had to do something about it.

"Do we have to do it tonight?" she asked.

"If we put it off until tomorrow morning, Gladys will be on duty. Do you really want to quiz Trish about the woman while she's in the back cooking?"

"No, you're right," Grace said. "Reach into the glovebox, would you? I have some antacid in there. I ate entirely too much tonight. It was just so good, I couldn't help myself."

"Mind if I join you?"

"You'd be a fool not to," she said.

Somehow we made the drive back to April Springs safely, but that just meant that we had to face Trish tonight after all. I knew if we didn't do it then, I'd toss and turn all night until we had another opportunity, but that didn't mean I was happy about what we were about to do.

We didn't have any choice, though.

Some hard questions had to be asked.

CHAPTER 13

UNFORTUNATELY, THE BOXCAR GRILL WAS crowded when we got there. "Suzanne, we can't do this now," Grace said.

"If we don't, it's not going to be easier later," I said. I approached Trish and asked, "Do you have a second?"

"Not really," she said as she looked around. "Is it important?"

"No, it can wait until things slow down. Whenever you're ready, Grace and I will be outside."

Trish's eyebrows shot up, but she didn't ask any more questions. "Give me ten minutes. I should have a little time then."

"How can you possibly know that?" Grace asked her.

"This place has a certain rhythm to it if you know how to read it," she said with a grin.

"We'll be out front," I said.

Once Grace and I were back outside, we commandeered a bench where customers sometimes waited when the diner was too busy. Night was beginning to fall, and a chill was definitely creeping into the air. We'd officially put winter behind us, but it was tough to believe it based on the weather.

Since we had a lull, I asked Grace, "Do you mind if I check in with Jake?"

"Go right ahead," she said.

I called, and he picked up on the third ring. "Hey, Suzanne." He sounded tired, and I wondered how he was holding up.

"How are things going there?" I asked him.

"Slow," he said. "I'm having a tough time tracking this guy down, and I used to be a cop. All I can say for sure right now is that he's not one of the good ones."

"How are Sarah and the kids doing?"

"Sarah's a wreck, Paul is angry, and Amy is trying to pretend that everything is okay here. It's not, though."

"Should I have come with you?" I asked. I hated that Jake might need me, and here I was back in April Springs trying to solve a murder. I had my own set of priorities, but had I let Sarah's aloofness toward me deter me from supporting my husband?

"It's not that I wouldn't love having you here, but I'm not sure it would help the situation," he said. "After the kids went to bed last night, Sarah and I stayed up past midnight talking. She knows what she's doing is not healthy for her or her kids, and I think she's finally going to turn things around. I just hope she can manage to do it. You believe people can change, don't you?"

"Absolutely," I said. I knew that it was difficult, and not many folks managed to accomplish it even if they were sincere about turning over a new leaf, but deep in my heart, I believed that most people wanted to do the right thing, especially where their kids were concerned, and no matter how Sarah might have felt about me, I knew that she loved her kids more than life itself.

"I do, too, regardless of what I've seen in the past," Jake said. "Thanks, you chose the exact right time to call me with a pep talk. How are things going there?"

I brought him up to speed on Gray's life before he came to April Springs. "What do you think of that?" I asked him.

"Chief Grant is probably right. I don't blame him for focusing on Mickey Wright. He's most likely the killer. Are you and Grace okay with being relegated to the second team?"

"Are you kidding? That's where we flourish. We're about to brace Trish about Gladys," I told him.

"I don't envy you that," Jake said.

"Well, I wouldn't trade you even, either, if that helps," I said. "It appears we've both got our work cut out for us."

"Sure, but if it was easy, everybody would be doing it," he said with a soft laugh.

I was about to reply when Trish came out. "Sorry, but I've got to go," I said.

"Love you," he said quickly.

"Love you, too," I replied.

Trish was frowning. "What's this about? It's got to be bad, or you both wouldn't still be here."

"Not necessarily," I said.

"Is this about Gladys?" she asked.

"It is," Grace admitted.

"I saw you talking to her this morning before her lunch shift. When I asked her what you were discussing, she didn't want to talk to me about it. Is it possible that you two are harassing one of my cooks?"

"Just the opposite. We're trying to help her," I said.

"Funny, you've got an odd way of showing it," Trish answered.

"Whether any of us like this or not, she's a suspect in Gray's murder. We're doing our best to eliminate her, but we need help doing it."

"Does Stephen Grant think she's a suspect, or is this just coming from the two of you?" Trish asked pointedly.

"He knows what we're doing, and he approves of it," Grace said.

"Officially?" Trish asked.

"You know that he can't do that, but he's not trying to stop us," I explained.

"So then the answer to that question is no," Trish said. "Why would Gladys kill him? *She* broke up with *him*, remember? It doesn't make sense."

"Money could be a factor," Grace said softly. There were many times when I needed Grace to be bold in our questioning. I tended to be a little too aware that no one had any obligation to speak with us, but Grace seemed to be able to act as though we were entitled to answers, even when we weren't.

"Are you saying that she *robbed* him?" Trish asked, growing angrier by the moment. "Just because her niece is in trouble doesn't mean that she'd kill someone to save her!"

"What's going on with her niece?" I asked.

Trish realized she'd spoken too quickly. "Forget I said that."

"We all know that we can't do that," I said. "So you might as well tell us. We'll find out anyway, and you don't want us asking embarrassing questions, do you?"

"Whose side are you on, Suzanne?" Trish asked me, hurt starting to show in her eyes.

"At the moment, I'm on Gray's," I said. "After all, he's not around to defend himself."

That took a little of the steam out of her. "I'm sorry he was murdered, but Gladys didn't have anything to do with it."

"Are you offering her an alibi?" Grace asked her.

Trish frowned before she spoke. "I wish I could, but after she made her presentation, I'm guessing that she watched the movie along with the rest of town. I didn't see her."

"It might help if she sat with someone who could verify that," I said.

"It won't do any good. She was so anxious about the fundraiser, she kept to herself; at least that's what she told me."

"So, no one can vouch for her whereabouts for an hour and a half," I said. It was clearly enough time for her to spot Gray leaving, follow him, kill him, and then return to the movie before anyone knew that she was gone. Unfortunately, the same could be said for any of our suspects. But had Barry, Donald, or

Mickey even been at the show? We needed alibis from the folks on our list.

"Not that she's aware of," Trish said. "Listen, I know you two are just trying to see justice done here, but Gladys isn't involved, so you need to drop it, unless you have more concrete proof that she might have done it."

"Tell her, Suzanne," Grace prompted me. "She has a right to know."

"Tell me what?" Trish asked sharply.

"I saw some paperwork when we were in Donald Rand's office earlier. It listed the beneficiary to Gray's financial account."

Trish's lips pursed into a single line before she spoke. "Don't tell me Gladys was set to inherit his money. How much could that amount to? He was practically a hermit, living in a small cabin in the woods by himself."

"Evidently he had quite a bit that no one knew about," I said.

"And Gladys is going to inherit it all now that he's dead?"

"We aren't sure," I said. "There were two names on those documents: Gladys's, and Donald Rand's as well."

"If you ask me, he's a lot more likely to have done it than her," Trish said.

"We think so, too, and we're pursuing that angle as well. But like it or not, Gladys is involved in this, and the sooner we clear her name, the quicker we can find the real killer." I said it, but I didn't entirely believe it. Now that we knew that Gladys had a pressing need for money as well as the opportunity to kill Gray Vincent, she had to be right up there near the top of our list, no matter how much we might have liked her.

Grace shot a quick glance at me, but I ignored her and kept my focus on Trish. She was about to say something when the door to the diner opened. Bert Gentry popped his head out. "Is somebody going to take my money, or was dinner on the house tonight?"

"I'm coming," Trish said. As she mounted the steps, she turned to look at me. "We're not through with this by any means, but I can't talk about it tonight."

"We'll be around," I said softly. "Trish, I hope this doesn't come between us."

"So do I," she said gravely.

After she went back inside, Grace said, "That didn't go very well, did it?"

"I don't know. We learned that Gladys is in need of money, and from the sound of it, a lot of it. If Gray came clean and told her that he was fairly well off, she might have acted on it, not out of self interest, but trying to help someone she cares about."

"I'm sorry. I still can't see it," Grace said. "It just seems out of character for her to stab a man in the chest, not to mention tying him up in the first place. How could she even manage to do that?"

"If she had the knife in her hand and Gray thought she was serious about stabbing him, he might have let her tie him up until he could calm her down," I said.

"Wow, do you think she actually might have done it?" Grace asked me.

"I'm not going to rule her out just because she's always been nice to us," I answered. "We've both seen seemingly nice people do some pretty outrageous things in the past."

"I know, but all things being equal, I'd rather it were someone we didn't like," she said a little wistfully.

"Believe me, I'd love to be able to hang this on one of the men, too. It would be wonderful if the chief were able to prove that Mickey Wright did it. If that fails, we've still got Donald Rand and Barry Vance."

"Donald might steal the change from your pocket, and Barry

could easily filch your postcard, but do you see either one of them as a killer?"

"We both know that our gut feelings aren't always right," I said. "All we can do is follow our leads, hunt for clues, interview our suspects, and see where the trail leads us."

"Sometimes I wish we could read minds," Grace said as we headed back to her place. "It would be so much easier spotting the killers that way."

I shuddered at the thought. "You can wish for that if you'd like, but I'm happy I don't know what people are thinking. Can you imagine the chaos? I'd never be able to live within a mile of anyone else."

"Like Gray?" she asked. "After years of living in a self-imposed exile, he tried to reach out and find love with Gladys, but in the end, all he had was his garden, and I can't imagine that was enough."

"I can't, either. Regardless, I think we're finished for the night. I don't know where to find Barry Vance or Donald Rand at this time of evening, and for now, we've done all that we can with Gladys, so where does that leave us?"

"We could always sneak out to Gray's house and have another look around the place," Grace suggested.

"It's an active crime scene," I reminded her. "I'm not sure Chief Grant would appreciate us traipsing through it."

"Maybe he's through with it," she suggested.

Knowing how the police worked, I seriously doubted it. "There's not one chance in a thousand that they're already finished there."

"Maybe not, but isn't that one hope worth driving out? Besides, it's too early for bed, even on your schedule."

"Sure, why not?" I asked. "Especially since I can't think of anything else to do."

"That's the spirit," Grace said with a grin.

It turned out that I had been right. At the gate that led into Gray's property, a cop was stationed protecting the entrance. Grace rolled down her window when we got there, much to my surprise. "Hey, Murph. Is the chief around?" she asked him.

"No, ma'am. He's handling something out on the highway. Do you want me to call him for you?"

"No, I'll catch up with him later. Have a good night."

"You, too."

"What was that all about?" I asked her once we'd turned around and headed back to her place.

"Officer Murphy was going to tell Stephen that we were out there, whether I stopped or not. This way we've got a reasonable excuse for snooping around."

"What makes you think he's going to call his boss and tell him anything?" I asked.

Grace held up three fingers as she counted down, "Three, two, one."

Nothing happened.

"That would have been so cool if it had worked," Grace said, just as her phone rang.

She answered, saying, "Hey. No, nothing to report just yet. Sure. Okay. Tomorrow sounds good." After she ended the call, she grinned at me. "Do I know my man or what?"

"Impressive indeed," I said. "That was smart thinking."

"I appreciate that. Now, since we're finished investigating for tonight, what would you like to do with the rest of our evening?"

"I've got another good hour in me, but after that, we both know that I'm going to nod off and fall asleep on your couch," I said.

"I'd be disappointed if you didn't," she said.

As we got back into town, my cellphone rang.

It was Phillip Martin, former chief of police and my current stepfather. I told Grace who was calling.

"I wonder what he wants?" she asked.

"There's only one way to find out," I said as I answered the call.

CHAPTER 14

"**H**EY, PHILLIP. IS EVERYTHING ALL right with Momma?" It was my first reaction whenever I heard from him directly. My mother was healthy and fit, but she wasn't getting any younger, and I was beginning to wonder how much time I had left with her. I'd taken her for granted over the years, but after my divorce and both of our remarriages, I'd finally understood how lucky I was to have her in my life. I didn't see her every day, as I had when we'd shared the cottage where I now lived with Jake, but I made it a point not to go too long without spending a little time with her.

"She's fine," he said. "I need to talk to you."

"Okay. What's up?"

"It's about Gray Vincent," he said. "I know it's approaching your bedtime, but do you have time to come by the house? There's something I'd like to show you."

"Sure. Grace and I will be there in three minutes," I said.

As I ended the call, Grace said, "I assume we've had a change in plans. Should I head over to your mother's place?"

"That would be great. Phillip has something he wants to share with us about Gray," I said. "It might not be anything, but you never know."

"Hey, we were just hoping for something to do. What could it hurt? Besides, it will be nice seeing your mother again. It's been ages since the last time I saw her."

"I was just thinking the same thing," I said.

When we got there, though, my mother wasn't at home.

"Where's Momma?" I asked him as I looked around the living room.

"She had a business meeting in Union Square this evening," he said. "She won't be back for hours. Is it okay that I called you?"

"Certainly. What do you know about Gray?"

He smiled. "Gray Vincent not so much, but Gary Manchester is another story altogether. I've been doing some digging around, and I found out a few things that you might find interesting."

"I thought your research was limited to old newspapers stored in dark basements," I said. The former police chief had become a bit of a history buff since he'd retired, and, no surprise, he'd focused most of his attention on crimes committed in the past.

"I've scanned through more than my share of those, but with the Internet, there's a great deal of information more available, and a lot easier to access, too." He frowned a moment before adding, "In the interest of full disclosure, you should know that I've already shared this information with Chief Grant. It was at his request that I did some digging into Manchester's past. Once I passed this information on to him, I asked for his permission to share it with you, which he granted."

"I appreciate you thinking of us at all," I said.

He looked at me carefully, as though he were trying to discern whether I was being sarcastic or not. I wasn't, but I couldn't blame him for his reaction. After all, the two of us had a long history of clashing in the past when he'd been in charge of April Springs's law enforcement, but since he'd married my mother and retired from the job, we'd finally found a way to coexist peacefully. "Happy to do it. Manchester was interesting, but it took some digging to find much out about him. Officially, he kept a pretty low profile, and there might not have been much about him to uncover if it weren't for one thing."

He grinned as he clearly waited for me to ask. "What was that?" I was happy to oblige.

"One of his former cohorts decided to come clean and confess every wrong he'd ever committed, seeking atonement for his past sins. He was dying of cancer, so he decided he needed to unburden his soul before it was too late. He wasn't very smart about it, though. Instead of talking to a priest, or even the police, he wrote an ebook about his past crimes, implicating several of his associates, including Manchester. Apparently, twenty years ago he was in on a private heist that should have lasted him for life, but he found a way to lose it all."

"We've already heard this story from the chief," I said.

Phillip nodded in understanding. "It figures. I don't blame him for telling you about it first. Anyway, I thought you should know."

It was clear that my stepfather was disappointed that he wasn't the one to break the news to us, so I decided to give him a chance to shine. "He just hit the main points with us, though. He told us about the robbery, the son getting killed, the collector having a heart attack, and the insurance company buying the paintings back."

"That's about it, then," Phillip said. "Did he tell you the crook turned author is dead?"

"No, we hadn't heard that," I said, suddenly interested. "What happened? Did the cancer finally catch up with him?"

"All I've been able to find out is that he died in his sleep. Whether he had help, I couldn't say."

"Do you think Mickey Wright found out about the ebook and killed him?" Grace asked.

"You know about Wright as well?" Phillip asked, clearly surprised that we had that much information.

"We've actually spoken with him," I admitted.

"Suzanne, from what I've been able to find out, he's a pretty nasty piece of work. You need to be really careful around him."

"We are, I promise," I said. "Has the chief told you everything about the case?" I wanted to know if Phillip knew about the missing cash as well, but I didn't want to say anything unless I knew.

"Yes, I'm working as a consultant for him. I'm sure he would have rather had Jake, but I was all he had."

"I wouldn't take it personally," I said. "Jake was quite a star with the state police."

"You don't have to tell me that. I'm guessing you're asking me about a bit of money, aren't you?"

"Two hundred thousand in cash is more than a bit, wouldn't you say?"

He nodded. "I would."

"What do you think happened to it?" Grace asked him.

"It's either still hidden, or somebody else stole it," the chief said.

"What happens if we find it?" I asked. "The chief said that the collector and his last known relative are both dead. Does it go back to the insurance company?"

"I don't see how it could," Phillip said. "There's no way to prove that any of Gray's money came from them, or any other robbery. As far as the law is concerned, it's his, and he came by it honestly."

"So, the investments Gray still had with Rand are considered clean," I said. That made the rightful heir to the man's money an active player on the scene.

"I can't imagine anyone being able to dispute it," he replied.

So then even if the killer didn't get the two hundred thousand in cash, there was still an equal amount coming to someone, which made it just as much a motive for murder as the cash.

"I suppose that makes sense," I said. "My next question is what tipped Mickey Wright off that his former associate was now living in our town under an assumed name?"

"Who knows? Maybe Gray got in contact with someone from his past life."

"He was much too careful for that," I said. "Unless."

"Unless what?" my stepfather asked.

"Unless he was reaching out to make amends himself," I finished.

"Would he do that?"

"He might, if he was trying to convince someone that he'd changed," I said.

"There's another possibility. Someone could have spotted him and followed him back here," the chief suggested. "I know the man lived like a hermit most of the time, but he came to town occasionally, and he even went to Charlotte every once in a blue moon. It may have just been his bad luck to be seen on one of the rare times he left his homestead. Chief Grant will have to ask Wright after he catches up with him."

"Do you think he's still in town?" Grace asked him.

"I don't have any proof that he is or he isn't, but if you two saw him *after* Manchester was murdered, then he clearly hasn't found what he was looking for yet. My gut tells me that he's still around."

"Do you have anything else for us?" I asked him.

The former chief of police shut his computer down as he faced me. "No, that's about it. If it hadn't been for that true confession published on the Internet, I would have had a great deal less. I sent a link for the ebook to the police chief, but I looked over it myself, too. The only name I could find was Mickey Wright's, but that doesn't mean that someone else isn't in town under a pseudonym as well. It's not as difficult to create a new identity as you might think, especially back then before we got so computerized and connected. Anyway, I hope it helps."

Grace pulled out her cellphone. "Would you mind telling me the title of that book?"

"Not at all," Phillip said.

After Grace had the title, she tapped a few times on her screen. "Got it."

"Did you write it down in your phone somewhere?" he asked.

"No, I bought it. I figure I can browse through it tonight. Who knows? It might help us somehow."

"Good luck. I'll tell you one thing; that book needs more than a good editor; it needs a complete overhaul."

"I'm not going to be reading it for the story," Grace said with a grin.

"If you manage to get through it without nodding off more than twice, you're a better person than I am," he said.

"Thanks for the information, but we'd better get going. Tomorrow is going to be here soon enough."

"I don't know how you're going to manage going to work at the donut shop on such little sleep," he said.

I didn't want to tell him that I was off for the next few days. After all, he might want us to linger, and I wanted to get back to Grace's so we could discuss what we'd just learned.

"She's off tomorrow," Grace supplied happily.

"That's great," the chief said. "Does that mean you two have time for a cup of tea?"

I couldn't back out gracefully. "We'd be glad to."

Something must have given away my disappointed acceptance, because he quickly added, "On second thought, you two are probably chomping at the bit to dig into that book. I'll give you a raincheck."

He wasn't a bad guy, and even if I hadn't been able to see that for myself, the fact that my mother had fallen in love with him should have been enough for me. "Thanks. I appreciate that."

"One last thing," he said before we could go.

Rats. I'd hoped we were going to make a clean escape. "What's that?"

"You've got a trained police officer at your disposal if you ever need some advice, or even just a sounding board."

"Jake's out of town," I said, "and we hate to bother the mayor with this."

"I meant me," he said, trying to hide the fact that I'd dinged his pride a little.

"I'm not sure Momma would approve of us getting you involved," I said with the hint of a grin, trying to make up for it.

"What she doesn't know won't hurt her, though," he answered, matching my smile with one of his own.

"It's just a bit complicated," I amended.

He shrugged. "I figured you'd react that way, but I thought I'd make the offer anyway. Happy hunting."

"Thanks," I said.

Once Grace and I were back out in her car, she said, "Sorry about that. I realized that I should have kept my mouth shut the moment I mentioned that you were off tomorrow."

"No worries," I said. "Deep down, he's really not a bad guy, is he?"

"The fact that you could say that given your history with him simply amazes me," Grace said with a laugh.

"People can change," I said in my defense.

"Including you," she said.

"What do you mean?"

"Suzanne, for the last several years, you've grown and blossomed into quite a woman. When you were married to Max, he always tended to overshadow you, something that killed me to see. After the divorce, when you bought the donut shop and moved back in with your mother, I was afraid for you, but you managed to make yourself stronger, and marrying Jake has just intensified that. It was almost as though it took something dark in your life to bring out the best in you."

"I don't know if I should thank you or not for that comment," I said.

"You should, by all means. It was the biggest compliment I could pay you."

I patted her arm. "Then thanks."

"You're most welcome. Should we go back to my place and read this book?"

"Do you think it could possibly be as bad as Phillip implied?" I asked her.

"There's only one way to find out. Tell you what.

Let's read it aloud to each other. We can alternate

Chapters and see if we can learn anything else about Gray Vincent, or Gary Manchester, as the case may be."

We did just that, reading it aloud to each other, trying to make it more dramatic and interesting than it really was. For all intents and purposes, the author had led an exciting life of crime, and yet he'd found a way to make it as boring as reading a telephone book. The parts about our old friend were interesting, but they didn't add anything to what the police chief or Phillip had told us earlier. We should have taken their words for it earlier, but Grace and I liked to think of ourselves as thorough. "I wonder if that cash is still hidden somewhere on his property?"

"It is unless someone already found it," Grace said.

"If we believe that's true, then Mickey Wright didn't do it."

"True, but worse news for us, that means that chances are good that one of our fellow residents did. Not only do we need to discover which one of our suspects committed the murder, but we also have to determine whether they found the cash or not."

"I'd think whoever did it would have a hard time just sitting around on that kind of money," I said. "The urge to run away must be really strong in them about now. Think about it. They not only committed a murder in cold blood, but they also stole enough to start a new life just about anywhere."

"How many folks do you know could stay in April Springs, given those facts?"

"I guess we'll see," I said. "If the killer *is* still in town, I say we add to their worries."

Grace smiled. "I'm all for doing that. Any suggestions about how we should go about doing that?"

"I say we start putting some real pressure on all three of them. Let's imply that we know more than we really do."

"It's not like we haven't done that before," Grace agreed. "But Trish isn't going to like us strong-arming Gladys."

"Maybe not, but we can't just ignore her. There are too many reasons to think that she might have actually done it."

Grace shook her head. "I still can't believe it."

"I'm having a tough time of it myself, but what choice do we have?"

"None," she said. "Should we figure out how we're going to pressure each of them?"

"Sure, why not?" I asked as I stifled a yawn. I glanced at the clock and saw that ordinarily, it would be well past my bedtime. I didn't know which was harder, getting up at the same dreadful hour every day, or only doing it five days a week. It was probably the latter. After all, a body can get used to just about anything, but changing a routine just enough to keep from getting used to it was deadly. I'd toyed with the idea of taking the donut shop back over seven days a week, but that wouldn't be fair to Jake, Emma, or Sharon. My husband liked having more time with me, and the mother-and-daughter team had grown used to the added income the new arrangements provided. That meant that I had a little less money than I was used to, but I still managed to squeak by. I wasn't sure how long I could keep doing it, though. One extended drought in sales would be enough to force me to take the shop back over full time, but until that happened, I was most likely just going to keep things the way they were. "Any ideas?" I asked her, stifling yet another yawn.

"Yes. You need to go to bed," Grace said.

"I'm not even all that sleepy," I said as I fought to make myself alert.

"Tell it to the judge," Grace said. "Off to bed, young lady."

"You're probably right. I am kind of beat."

"And why wouldn't you be? Not only are you a full-time donutmaker, but you're fighting crime on the side as well. It's enough to exhaust anyone."

"Thanks for understanding. I'll see you at five." It was the latest I'd been able to sleep on my days off. That wasn't usually a problem though, since Jake awoke that time of morning every day, whether he had a job or not.

"In the morning?" Grace asked as she looked at me incredulously. "You might be up then, but I'm not rolling out of bed until seven, and even that's a concession to you. I may have taken the next few days off work myself, but that doesn't mean that I'm getting up while it's still dark outside, for goodness sake."

"What should I do while I'm waiting for you to wake up?" I asked her with a grin.

"Make pancakes, do a crossword puzzle or two, repaint the porch; I don't care. Just don't wake me up."

"It's a deal. I'll see you in the morning," I said as I went into her guestroom.

"Remember, not too early," she said with a soft smile. It may have given someone who didn't know her the impression that she'd been kidding about me not waking up her up before seven, but for anyone who knew her, they'd realize that Grace was deadly serious.

"Not too early," I echoed.

It always takes me a while to fall asleep in a strange place, even if it was only steps from my own bed back at the cottage. As I lay there trying my best to will myself to sleep, I thought about Jake. How was he really doing with his sister and her no-good boyfriend? I knew that he'd be happy to spend time with Sarah's kids, but would Paul and Amy be enough to take his mind off the situation his sister had gotten herself into yet again? I considered calling him, but I wasn't sure I wanted to know if things were going poorly on his end, too.

Selfishly, I decided that I wouldn't be of any help to him, and it would just delay my slumber that much longer. Forcing out the thought of my husband being so many miles away, and the fact that a killer was ever so much closer, I did my best to fall asleep, and to my surprise, twenty minutes later, I finally managed to do just that.

CHAPTER 15

"**H**EY, SLEEPYHEAD," I SAID THE next morning as Grace finally came out of her bedroom.

She looked blearily at the clock. "It's four minutes past seven," she said. "Coffee. Must have coffee."

I'd made a fresh pot, so I poured her some. She smelled the aroma wafting from her mug before sipping it. "That's delightful. Are those for me?"

"You mentioned pancakes earlier," I said, "so I thought I'd make some."

"You didn't have to do that," she said, "but I'm glad you did." She took one from the plate and studied it a moment. "This doesn't look like my usual pancake."

"That's because I added some diced apple, instant oatmeal, raisins, vanilla, nutmeg, and cinnamon to your mix," I said.

She looked at the pancake skeptically. "I'm not sure about this."

"Put a little butter on it and dash some syrup on top and try it," I said. "If you don't like it, I'll make some with the plain mix you had in your pantry."

"Okay. I'm going to hold you to that," she said as she did as I'd instructed. After cutting off a tiny edge, she ate it, chewing slowly and carefully. "I can't taste any oatmeal in it, but I can sure tell there's apple."

"Did I use too much?" I asked her.

"No, it's perfect." Grace took another bite, and then she smiled. "That's actually delicious. Care to join me?"

"Thanks, but I already ate," I said, and then I took a sip of my own coffee.

"Where did you learn to make these?" she asked me.

"I've been doctoring my pancake mix for years," I admitted. "You just happened to have an apple in your pantry, and some quick oats and raisins, too."

"Wow, you truly are the wizard of breakfast, aren't you?" Grace asked after taking a few more bites.

"Yes, I've found my niche in life," I said good-naturedly.

"That wasn't a slam, Suzanne," she said as she took another bite. She'd polished off one pancake and was starting on another, so I knew that she really must like them.

"I didn't take it as such," I said. "After you finish eating, let's start tracking down our suspects and see if we can make them squirm."

"Sounds like fun to me," she said as she polished off her last small segment.

"Don't feel as though you have to eat them all," I said. "They freeze great, and they'll make a handy snack."

"Okay, you're right," she said as she pushed her plate away. "If I eat any more, I'll be waddling around the rest of the day, anyway. Give me half an hour to get ready, and we can get started."

As she stood, I started clearing the table.

"You don't have to do that," she said.

"I don't mind," I replied. "I'm used to cleaning up as I go, so this won't take much time at all."

"Thanks," Grace said with a smile. "You're like the perfect houseguest, you know? Would you care to stay again tonight?"

"It might not be a bad idea, if the situation doesn't improve," I said, running some water in her sink. She had a dishwasher, but I didn't want to leave the few things behind for her to deal with later, even if it just meant running it through its cycle and putting the clean dishes away.

"It's a deal. And about tomorrow morning."

"What about it?" I asked. Was she going to invite me out to eat breakfast in return for feeding us this morning? Not quite.

"I have some canned pumpkin in the cupboard. How would that be in the pancake mix?"

I laughed. "I've done that, too. They're really good."

"Yum. I can hardly wait."

As we got into Grace's car half an hour later, I fought the urge to direct her toward my cottage instead of toward town. For some reason, I felt the urge to make sure that it was still there, intact and unharmed. I knew that I was being unreasonable, but the desire was there nonetheless. I got over it by the time we got to the donut shop, and I was happy to see that the parking area in front of the shop was full, and there was a line of customers queued up inside.

Grace must have noticed it, too. "Do you want to go in and lend them a hand?"

"No, I'd better not," I said absently before I looked over at her. "You were kidding, weren't you?"

"Suzanne, I know how hard it is for you to let go of your baby. I'm proud of you for doing it as much as you've managed to do so far."

"It hasn't been easy," I said. "Who should we tackle first?"

"Well, I'm guessing that Donald Rand isn't in the office yet, and Gladys is probably still at home. That leaves Barry Vance. He's probably out on his route already, but I have no idea how we find him."

"There's only one thing we can do," I suggested. "We drive around until we spot him, or something else that might grab our attention."

"What I'd really like to do is go snoop at Gray's place," Grace said.

"I'd like to do that myself, but chances are good that if there was a cop posted on duty last night, there will be one there this morning."

"Tell you what we should do. If we drive around and can't find Barry, and if it's still too early to visit Rand or Gladys, then we try out there again. What do we have to lose?"

"That sounds like a solid plan to me," I said.

We got lucky, which was a nice change of pace. Barry was just leaving the post office for his rounds. He was dressed in his uniform, shorts included, and was pushing a cart with his day's deliveries.

Unfortunately, he wasn't alone.

"Barry, do you have a second?" I asked him after Grace had pulled over and found a place to park. We'd gotten ahead of him, so we were waiting when he approached.

"Sorry, I'm busy," he said brusquely.

"It's important," I said, and then I looked at the young woman with him, also wearing the same blue uniform, though she looked much better in it than Barry did. "Hi there, I'm Suzanne Hart."

I extended a hand, and she took it and smiled. "I'm Kimberly Atkins," she said.

"I'm training her," Barry said.

"New to the job?" Grace asked her.

"I've been working in Union Square, but when this route opened up, I jumped on it."

"You're not quitting, are you, Barry?" I asked him.

"It's not common knowledge," he said as he glared at his

trainee, "but I've served my time. If I don't walk another step on this beat after tomorrow, that will be just fine with me."

"Did you qualify for your pension already?" Grace asked. It was an excellent question, one I hadn't thought to ask.

"Don't worry about me. I'm all set," he said.

"But I thought you were still six months away from getting it in full," Kimberly said, clearly puzzled by his answer.

"There are more things to life than money. I'm leaving April Springs and moving in with my sister and her family down in Big Pine Key, Florida. They have a guest cottage nobody's using, so I've finally decided to take her up on her offer to come down there. Now if you'll excuse me, we've got work to do, if you don't mind."

"We don't mind a bit," I said. "Just one more question, though. How are you going to be able to afford to live down there without your full pension?"

"I won't need much," he said. "Besides, that's not really any of your business, is it?"

As they walked away, I said, "It was nice meeting you, Kimberly. Welcome to April Springs. If you get a chance, come by Donut Hearts, and I'll treat you to a free donut."

"That sounds wonderful," she said.

"Let's go," Barry said as he sped up his pace. It was as though he couldn't get away from us fast enough.

After they were gone, I asked Grace, "What do you make of that?"

"I don't buy it. I've never known a civil servant to leave their job so close to qualifying for their full pension. Something's up."

"If he killed Gray and stole that cash, he wouldn't need any more money for quite a while, would he?" I asked her as I watched them turn the corner.

"Does he even *have* a sister living in the Florida Keys?" Grace asked me.

"Beats me. Maybe we should ask around."

"Agreed, but we need to do it quickly. If he's leaving day after tomorrow, our time is running out," Grace said. "What now?"

I glanced at my watch. "Do you think there's a prayer that Donald Rand is in his office by now?"

"The market doesn't open for a while yet, but he might be in early. It won't hurt anything to check and see."

"Let's walk over there," I said. "It's a pretty morning, and besides, I could use the exercise. I've been sampling too many of my goodies lately."

"I'm fine with that," Grace said.

I admired her slim shape yet again. "How do you manage it?"

"Manage what?"

"To stay so fit."

"It's easy. If I gain more than two pounds, most of my business suits won't fit. It's a perfect reminder that it's time to cut down on my treats when the buttons get harder to fasten. I've got it a lot easier than you do."

"How so?"

"I'm around makeup all day, which, the last time I checked, was nonfattening. You, on the other hand, live your life around pastry treats. I'm just amazed you've managed to keep your figure, given all of that."

"I keep it all right, and I even add to it," I answered with a smile. "I have an easy solution to your suit problem."

"I'm listening," she said.

"Buy a bigger size. That's what I do with my jeans."

Grace laughed. "No offense, but my work clothes cost a little more than yours do."

"None taken," I said with a grin.

We were approaching Donald Rand's office on the outskirts of town, and I saw something on his door. As we neared it, I could see that it was a message. *"We are closed for the foreseeable future. To get in touch with me about your investments, call 555-3154."*

I pulled out my phone.

"What are you doing?"

"I'm calling the number," I said. I dialed the digits posted, but instead of getting Rand, I heard a recorded message. *"This number is no longer in service and is not currently a working number. Please check the listing again and redial. Thank you."*

I dialed again, this time more carefully. Perhaps I'd transposed some of the digits, or even gotten one wrong entirely.

I got the same message again.

"You try it," I said.

Grace shrugged, pulled out her cellphone, and dialed.

"It's been disconnected," she said. "That's going to make it tough for his clients to get in touch with him, isn't it?"

"I don't get it. How can he just disappear like that?"

"I don't know, but I'm calling Stephen," she said. "He needs to know that one of our suspects has disappeared."

"Don't forget to tell him about Barry's plan to leave town, too," I said. "That's something else he needs to know."

Grace nodded as her call went through. As she caught her boyfriend up on what we'd discovered, I couldn't help wondering what was going on. Most likely the fact that two of our main suspects were leaving or had already left town was simply a coincidence, but I didn't believe it. Surely one of them was guilty of something. I didn't like the direction this thing was heading. If Rand was already gone, with Barry Vance soon to follow, what did that do to our investigation? Most of the information Grace and I had picked up in the past was from active interviews, and if we couldn't find our suspects, we couldn't very well question them.

Grace hung up. "He wants us to wait right here."

"Didn't you already tell him everything?" I asked him, not

that we had anywhere else we needed to be in a hurry. Gladys wasn't supposed to be at work for at least another hour, if her schedule was still the same. No doubt at this very moment, her fellow cook, Hilda, was at her station. But what if they changed their shifts? Were we wasting time waiting on Chief Grant when what we really should be doing was heading for the Boxcar Grill? "Why don't you wait for him, and I'll walk over to the Boxcar by myself?"

"You can't go without me," Grace protested. "He said he wouldn't be long."

"Okay," I agreed reluctantly. I wouldn't like it if she went off investigating without me, so I had to respect her request.

At least the chief was as good as his word. Three minutes after Grace had ended the call, he pulled in front of the financial man's office and got out. "Did either one of you know that he was leaving town all of a sudden?" he asked after he confirmed that the number was a dead one as well. I couldn't blame him. After all, I'd had Grace check behind me, too. It just didn't add up.

"We had no idea," I said.

"Maybe the attention you two were giving him spooked him," the chief said.

"I don't see how that's possible," I replied. "He seemed to handle our questions just fine."

"On the outside, maybe, but he's probably good at keeping his cool under pressure. You could have rattled him, especially if he had a guilty conscience."

"Where could he have gone?" Grace asked.

"I have no idea, but I'll put out a bulletin for law enforcement around here to be on the lookout for him. Thanks for letting me know."

"What about Barry Vance?" I asked him before he could get back into his car. "Are you going to talk to him as well?"

"The man's quitting his job, Suzanne. There's nothing inherently suspicious about that."

"What about his pension?" Grace asked. "He doesn't have that long to wait to get all of it, so why leave now?"

"I'll talk to him," the chief said reluctantly, "but it's been known to happen before. Didn't Jake quit being the police chief on an impulse?"

I wasn't at all certain how impulsive that had been. After all, it had been probably been brewing for some time, and finding his wife, her best friend, his mother-in-law, and the mayor himself staking out a suspect's house had most likely just been the last straw of many. "That's something entirely different," I said in Jake's defense.

"I didn't mean anything by it," he said. "I'll have a word with Vance before he leaves town."

"Good. That's all we're asking," I said.

He looked around. "Where's your car?"

"We left it on Springs Drive," Grace said.

"Well, hop in. Since I held you up, the least I can do is give you a ride back into the heart of town. What do you say?"

"Can we use the siren and lights on the way?" I asked him with a grin.

"No, and just for that, *you* have to sit in back," he said, smiling.

"As long as I don't have handcuffs on, we're good," I said. Grace got in front, and I headed for the backseat. Her view was better than mine. She had an unobstructed window, while I had wire mesh; she actually had a doorknob and a window crank, two things that were clearly lacking in my space.

At least it wouldn't be long.

With my luck, I glanced over and saw my mother driving in the opposite direction. She glanced casually into the backseat of the cruiser, saw me sitting there grinning at her, and nearly hit a light pole with her car!

My cellphone rang immediately.

"You need to be more careful there, Momma," I said happily before she could say anything.

"Suzanne, what have you done this time?" she asked.

I laughed. "Believe it or not, Grace and I are just catching a ride back to her car, but thanks for jumping to that conclusion so quickly."

"Can you blame me?" she asked. The relief in her voice was evident, and I couldn't really be mad at her. In fact, it was probably a reasonable thing to assume, given my history.

"No, not really. Sorry we missed you last night."

"Phillip told me all about it. How's your investigation going?"

"So far, we're hitting one dead end after another," I admitted.

"Well, don't give up. You and Grace are too good at this to stop now."

"I appreciate the vote of confidence," I said as we pulled up at the police station. "I've got to go now."

"Take care," she said.

"I will if you will. Watch that road now, you hear?"

"I can be forgiven this time. After all, it's not every day I see my daughter in the back of a police squad car," she said in her defense.

"No, but it's not that unexpected either, is it? Bye."

I was just telling Grace and Chief Grant what Momma had said when I noticed someone standing in front of the station, wringing her hands together.

Gladys Murphy was standing there impatiently, apparently waiting to speak with the chief of police.

She didn't know it yet, but there were going to be two more participants in the conversation, at least if I had anything to say about it.

CHAPTER 16

"I F YOU TWO WILL EXCUSE me, I'll handle this," Chief Grant said as we all started to get out of the car.

At least Grace had the option of leaving freely.

"I need a hand here," I said. "There's no doorknob, remember?"

He shrugged as he got out and unlocked my door and opened it for me.

Gladys rushed toward us. "Chief, I need to speak with you. It's important."

"Absolutely. Let's go into my office," the police chief said.

"Mind if we tag along?" I asked Gladys. I'd already gotten Chief Grant's opinion, but I figured Gladys might overrule him. Anyway, it was worth a shot.

"That's fine. It might be nice having a few friendly faces nearby when I tell this."

"What's wrong? I'm not a friendly enough face all on my own?" the chief asked her.

"Of course you are," she said, "but it's directly because of Suzanne and Grace that I'm even here. It's only fitting that they hear what I have to say."

"Then let's all go back and make ourselves comfortable," the chief said graciously.

Gladys was clearly not a fan of the idea. "I was in there earlier, so if you don't mind, I'd rather do this out here."

He was beyond fighting now. "Suit yourself. What's up?"

I braced myself for what Gladys was about to say. Were we about to hear a murder confession?

CHAPTER 17

"THERE'S SOMETHING YOU ALL NEED to know. I've kept it from you all too long."

"What do you need to tell us?" Chief Grant asked softly. He was doing his best to make it easy on Gladys, but I couldn't imagine what she might be about to tell us.

"It's my fault that someone killed Gray!" she said through her tears.

"What makes you say that?" I asked her, overstepping my bounds, but not caring. A friend was in pain, and I felt the urge to help her.

"When he told me that he had a dark past and hinted that he had a criminal record, I didn't even wait to hear the facts. I told him that I didn't want to have anything to do with him! He said he'd do anything to show me that he was a changed man. I told him to prove it, and he asked me how he could possibly do that. I said that he should go to the people he'd wronged and say that he was sorry. He told me that if he did that, it would be a death sentence for him. I thought he was exaggerating! He said that he couldn't make up for what he'd done, but he must have tried, and he was murdered for it! It's all my fault." Her sobs wracked her entire body now.

Without thinking, I rushed forward and embraced her, with Grace close behind me. We enveloped her in our arms, and after a full minute, we finally managed to calm her down. "It's okay, Gladys," I said. "It's not your fault."

"If I hadn't pushed him to make amends, none of this would have ever happened," she said, clearly a beaten woman.

"He was a grown man," Chief Grant said. "I doubt anyone could have made him do anything he didn't want to do. If he did act on what you said, that just proves that he really loved you. None of what happened was your responsibility."

"Then why can't I make myself believe it?" she asked.

"Did he ever say anything more specific about who he might need to apologize to?" the chief asked. He was interviewing her, but subtly, and I had to admire his technique.

"No," she said, drying the tears from her eyes. "We dropped it, and I just figured it was over. Then he found me during the movie and told me that he'd done as I'd asked. He'd tried his best to find the all of the people he'd wronged, but he couldn't find most of them. They were either dead, in prison, or missing. He begged me for another chance, but I refused. Me and my pride! How I wish I had that moment in time back. I would do things so differently!"

Nobody had anything to say to answer that. I stroked her arm, and after a few moments, she said, "Anyway, I just wanted you to know. I've got to get over to the diner."

"We'll walk you," I offered.

"I appreciate that, but I just want to be alone right now," she said as she drifted off in the general direction of her workplace.

"That was bad, wasn't it?" Grace asked.

"She's going to have a lot to deal with," the chief said.

"Is it true? Did she really cause all of this?" Grace asked hesitantly.

"If I had to guess, I'd say yes," the chief answered pragmatically.

"That's kind of harsh, isn't it?" I asked him.

He just shrugged. "I can't help it if it sounds that way to you. Maybe he reached out to the wrong person, and it cost him his life, too."

I caught that last bit, as subtle as it was. "Too? Was someone else murdered recently?"

"What? What are you talking about?" the chief asked. I'd clearly caught him revealing something that he didn't want exposed.

That's when I had a solid hunch what he was talking about. "The author of that ebook Phillip told us about didn't die of natural causes, did he? Someone helped him along. Am I right?"

He started to protest; I could see the words form on his lips, but finally, he threw up his hands. "Wow, remind me never to do anything wrong around you. It's possible. We just got word that the author might not have died of natural causes after all. My questions prompted the cops there to reexamine the case. He'd been diagnosed with cancer and was close to death, but there's a chance that someone couldn't wait that long for nature to run its course. They are going to exhume the body and retest it. After that, they'll contact me and tell me what they discovered."

"So, it's possible that someone else has died because of this," I said.

"Or not. It might be nothing," the chief reminded me.

"But you don't think so, do you? That's why you're after Mickey Wright, isn't it?"

"He's the only one of my suspects actively linked to the robbery way back when," he said. "It just makes sense, if that's the case."

"Have you had any luck tracking him down yet?" Grace asked him.

"We've had half a dozen leads, from him being holed up in the woods nearby to someone spotting him on the Outer Banks. We just don't know yet."

"I hope you find him, and soon," I said.

As I finished speaking, the chief's radio sprang into life. "Chief, are you there? Chief!"

It was one of his deputies. "What's up, Murphy?"

"Shots fired at the Vincent place! I was patrolling like you told me to, and the next thing I know, someone took a shot at me!"

"Take a deep breath," the chief said. "Were you hit?"

"No, he missed me, but I might have clipped him. He jerked a little when I fired, anyway."

"Did you get a good look at the suspect?" the chief asked as he opened his car door and jumped in.

"I might be wrong, but I could swear it was Mickey Wright!" he said.

"Any chance we can tag along?" I asked him.

"No, and don't follow me. I'll call you later, Grace."

"Be careful!" she yelled out, but he was already gone.

Perhaps our case, and the hunt for Gray Vincent's killer, was finally over.

CHAPTER 18

"SO, WHAT DO WE DO in the meantime?" I asked Grace after Chief Grant was gone. We started the short walk to where her car was parked. "Do we just give up and wait to see what happens at Gray's place?"

"I don't know. Is that what you want to do?"

"No," I said firmly, realizing that it was true. Even if Officer Murphy had shot Mickey Wright at Gray's house, it didn't necessarily mean that he had killed his old partner in crime. If he'd come searching for Gray's stash, a little thing like murder probably wouldn't get in his way. "I still have a hard time believing that he killed Gray," I told Grace.

"Why not? I'm willing to keep an open mind."

"Gray died too easily," I said, surprising myself by saying it.

"It didn't look all that easy to me," Grace said with a frown. "In fact, it looked like a pretty hard way to go."

"I'm not saying it was pleasant, but let's play this through in our minds. Let's say for a moment that Mickey Wright killed the partner who wrote the book, and then he came after Gray for his share. If they knew each other all that well in the past, he'd know that Gray was tight with his money, so there would be a good chance he still had a nice-sized chunk of it."

"Okay. But so what?"

"Grace, Gray was tied up and stabbed once. I imagine he died pretty quickly. Now think about it. If Mickey Wright did it, do you think there's a chance he wouldn't have put Gray through a lot more than that if he didn't know where that cash was hidden?"

Grace nodded. "And if he told Wright, there would be no reason to still be here in town searching for the loot. I see where you're going with this. That might mean that the ebook author rat may have died of natural causes after all. Do we wait until we get official confirmation one way or the other?"

"I'm still not sure it matters," I said.

"I'm guessing that it mattered to him."

"That's not what I mean. Something in my gut is telling me that Mickey Wright didn't kill Gray Vincent. If he did, it would have been sloppy of him to do it before he found out where Gray's stash was hidden."

"Okay. Let's go on the assumption that Mickey didn't do it. You're right. What does it hurt if we assume that much? Stephen has Mickey covered anyway. That leaves us with Gladys, Rand, and Barry Vance. We can't find Rand or Vance, and after what Gladys told Stephen, can you see her killing Gray, especially like that?"

"She might have poisoned him, but I doubt that she would have stabbed him, let alone tied him up like that first," I said.

Grace looked at me uncertainly. "Do you think that's even possible?"

"What? No. I'm just saying, with her working around food all the time, don't you think it would have been easy for her to pretend to make up with Gray, feed him a poison-laced meal, and then just watch while he ate it?"

Grace shivered a little. "That's kind of dark, Suzanne, even for you."

"I'm not suggesting that she did it. In fact, I don't think she killed anyone. She was too torn up by the fact that she'd pressed Gray into doing something he didn't want to do. There's no way she could have faked that, if you ask me."

"It's probably not enough to clear her of suspicion," Grace said.

"No, but it makes me want to focus more on Barry Vance and Donald Rand."

"Okay, but we can't find Donald, and Barry is clearly not in the mood to speak with us," Grace said.

"Are you talking about Donald Rand?" a voice asked from just behind us.

It was Gabby Williams. Evidently she'd been following us on foot from the police station. Just how much had she heard? "Gabby, what are you doing out walking? Are you having car problems?" I asked her.

"No, my doctor is insisting that I get more exercise, so I started walking to ReNEWed when the weather is nice. I heard you mention Donald's name. Why do you want to see him?"

"We have some things we need to discuss with him," I said, trying to be as vague as possible. Gabby wouldn't need much to start up a whirlwind of rumors about our search for the man, but I was determined not to feed her any information I didn't have to.

"We went by his office earlier," Grace said. "There was a note on the door that he'd be gone for a while, and when we tried to dial the listed number, we found out it had been disconnected."

Gabby was trying to hide it, but I could swear that I saw her smile a little before she stifled it. I asked her, "Gabby, what do you know that we don't?"

"There's not enough daylight left to cover that expansive ground," she said as she walked past us. "Excuse me, but I've got to get to my shop."

"We'll walk with you," I said as I motioned to Grace to follow as well. "Tell us about Donald."

"Well, the first thing is that the sign you saw is merely a ruse.

He's used it for years, and I know for a fact that the number he listed has never worked."

"Then why put it on the sign at all?" I asked.

"It gives his clients a sense that he's in touch, when it's the farthest thing from it. That's his hiding sign. We all have one. Don't you, Suzanne?"

"I have no idea what you're talking about," I said.

"Come now. There must be times when you don't want to see or speak to anyone. I know I do. When I'm in one of my moods, I put the sign up, turn off the lights, and spend some time in back until I'm feeling a bit more social."

I wouldn't have dreamed of doing that. "How do your customers react?"

"How can they? Surely you've noticed mine before. It says that I'm off buying inventory for the shop. Who can dispute that, or argue that I should be open around the clock?"

"And the entire time you've been cowering in back?" I asked, immediately regretting my choice of words. "I meant that you've been in seclusion," I amended quickly.

Gabby wasn't buying it. "The public doesn't own me, Suzanne. I thought you, of all people, would understand that."

"I do," I said hastily. "I just don't know how you can afford to do it."

"You're kidding, right? Once I open my doors again, folks stream in searching for my 'new finds'."

"But you don't have anything to show them," Grace noted.

"I've *always* got things in back. I rotate some of them out front, and no one has ever caught on yet."

"So, you think Donald is hiding in his office, despite what his sign says?"

Gabby laughed, enjoying having more information than I did. "I didn't say that, did I?"

This was getting frustrating, and what was more, we were

running out of space between where we were and where Gabby was heading. If we didn't get any useful information out of her by the time she crossed the threshold of her shop, it would take forever to get anything out of her. The only way I could turn things around was to make her an ally instead of an opponent. "What should I write on mine?" I asked her humbly.

"On your what?" Gabby asked, not following me. Grace looked puzzled too, but she stayed silent, something I greatly appreciated.

"My sign," I said. "I could really use your advice."

Gabby looked pleased by my request. "If I were you, I think I'd say something like, "Gone on a Supply Run", or perhaps "Fryer Broken" don't you think they would work?"

"I'll make one up this weekend," I said.

"Just don't overuse it, or folks might get suspicious."

I wasn't planning on using it at all, so that wasn't going to be a problem. "We know you're busy, but before you start your day, if you were looking for Donald Rand, where would you begin?"

"Try Union Square," she said with that mischievous twinkle back in her eye.

"It's a good-sized town," Grace said. "Can you narrow it down any?"

"Lolly's Pops," she said.

"The candy store? What would Donald Rand be doing there?"

"It's simple. He's sweet on the owner," Gabby said, smug that she'd said something clever.

"Seriously? I never would have thought that."

"That's why you have me," Gabby said as she unlocked her front door.

I couldn't let her go just yet. "How do you know about them?"

"I was in Union Square shopping a few months ago, and I noticed Donald going into the shop. It struck me as an odd place for him to be, but when I glanced inside, I saw him kiss

Evangeline Truitt with enough passion to melt the cotton candy. When I walked in, they pretended that nothing had happened between them, but her face was so red I was worried it might spontaneously combust."

"Did you ask Donald about it later?" Grace inquired.

"Of course not. That would ruin my fun."

"How is it fun?" Grace asked her.

"Him not knowing whether I saw them or not was what made it so delightful. Now off with you both. I have work to do."

"Thanks for the help, Gabby," I said.

"Any time. You know me; I'm always eager to please."

I nearly choked keeping myself from commenting, so I did my best to just smile and nod. Grace was amused, but not at Gabby. She was trying her best not to laugh at me.

Once Gabby was safely inside, Grace said, "I thought you were going to have a stroke there at the end."

"And you found that funny?" I asked her with a grin.

"I just wish I'd filmed it. I can't believe Donald Rand is seeing Evangeline Truitt."

"Do you know her very well?" I asked. I'd been aware of the candy store, but I didn't trust myself to go inside. After all, I had enough vices without adding candy to the list.

"I've been in a time or two," Grace admitted.

"Would she recognize you?"

"I should hope so," Grace replied.

"Then we have to go in without any cover story," I said. "All we can do is ask if Donald Rand is around and hope that she tells us the truth."

Once were in Union Square, Grace drove directly to the sweets shop. I was surprised to find it open to the public so early. Not only that, but the door leading to the back was partially open, and Donald Rand was sitting at a desk, staring at a computer screen.

"So there you are," I said as Grace and I walked into the shop together.

"I'm usually here," the woman behind the counter said, looking slightly perplexed.

"She wasn't talking to you, Evangeline," Rand said.

"Are these friends of yours?" the candy store owner asked him.

"Hardly," Rand said gruffly.

"Now, Donald. What did we just discuss?" She was scolding him like an old-fashioned schoolmarm, and I prepared myself for the blast I knew he was going to answer with.

But it never came.

Instead, in a submissive voice, he said, "Sorry about that. What can I do for you ladies?"

Was this the same Donald Rand I'd butted heads with in the past? He looked to be the same man, but he surely wasn't acting like it. "We saw the sign on your office door," I said with a grin, not even trying to hide it. "The number doesn't work."

"I thought you were going to fix that, Donnie," Evangeline said softly.

"Must have slipped my mind," he said quickly. "I'll take care of it when I get back." It was clear the financial planner didn't enjoy speaking with us in front of his lady friend. "Do you two want to step outside? There's no need to bother Evangeline with this."

"How are my books coming?" she asked him.

"They're getting there," he answered gently.

After we were outside, I couldn't help myself. "What's the deal, Donnie?"

He ignored my familiar use of his name. "What are you two doing here? I know you didn't just happen upon me by accident."

"Why not? It's possible," Grace said.

"Yes, but not very likely." He stewed about it for a few moments, and then his frown grew even deeper. "It was Gabby, wasn't it?"

"Gabby? Gabby Williams? How could she possibly know that we could find you here?" I asked him.

"Drop the act. I knew she spotted us before she walked in a few months ago, so of course she told you."

"Are you actually ducking out on your clients to do your girlfriend's books?" I asked him. It was hard for me to believe that Gabby and Donald both skipped out of their responsibilities so easily. It usually took an act of Congress to get me to do it.

"She's hopeless at it," Rand said. "If she's not rounding down, she's rounding up, and I'm not just talking about nickels and dimes, either. That's if she remembers to post the numbers at all. I'm ready to open a new account for her and start over, but I know how quickly it will lose any sense of accuracy at all."

"I think it's sweet," I said.

"Nice wordplay, Suzanne. Why are you two here?"

"We wanted to talk to you about Gray's murder," I said.

"Again? I didn't kill the man. I wasn't even in town when he died!"

I realized that we hadn't had a chance to ask anyone for their alibis yet. "Can you prove that?"

"It's simple enough. I was here with Evangeline," he said gruffly.

"Will she verify that?" I asked.

"The woman is incapable of lying!" Donald said fiercely. "Ask anybody. We were here all night while she made fudge, if you can call it that."

"So then it's true that opposites attract," Grace asked with a hint of a grin.

"What can I say? She's trying to make me a better man," Donald said.

"Against your wishes?" I asked.

"Let's just say that it's an ongoing process. Go on. Ask her."

Grace started to go in, but I stopped her. "One more thing first. When we were in your office earlier, there were papers on your desk naming a new beneficiary for Gray Vincent's investments. Who is going to receive that money?"

"I can't tell you that! It's confidential!"

"Your client is dead. Do you think he'd care at this point?" Grace asked. "Of course, we could always ask you in Evangeline's presence. I have a feeling you might be a little more cooperative then."

He clearly didn't like it, but Donald Rand said with a scowl, "Fine. What can it hurt at this point? It's going to be common knowledge soon enough."

"Are you inheriting it all yourself?" Grace asked him, clearly jumping the gun.

"What? No! Of course not."

"I saw your name on those papers, so don't bother trying to deny it," I said.

"Why wouldn't they be there? I was acting in Gray's behalf. I was never going to inherit anything from him. He was a client. You might not believe it, but I do have ethics."

"Does that mean that Gladys is getting the money?" I asked. I was afraid of the answer, but I needed to hear it nonetheless.

"No."

"But I saw her name on the documents, too," I protested.

"I'm not denying it, but there was just one little problem with those forms."

"What's that?" I asked.

"Gray never signed them," Donald Rand said with a shrug.

CHAPTER 19

"WHAT DO YOU MEAN, HE never signed them?" I asked.

"He had me draw up the papers, but then he told me to sit on them for a while."

"Why was that?" Grace asked.

"I asked him just that, and he told me that if Gladys accepted his proposal, then she'd get everything."

"And if she didn't?" I asked.

"Then the beneficiary he had listed before would stand," Donald Rand explained.

That led to another question. "Who gets it all now, then?"

"The April Springs Garden Club. He said in the end that it was only fitting that they end up with it," he said with a grimace. "Gray was nuts about flowers and landscaping. Have you ever seen his place?" He caught himself. "Of course you have. You two found his body. It's a shame, but what can you do? As soon as things settle out, that club is going to get a windfall they aren't going to believe. They'll get the two hundred grand I'm investing, and if the cash ever turns up, they'll get that as well. Gray was going to change his will, too, but Gladys said no."

I had a sudden thought. "Does anyone on the committee know what they're about to get?" I asked him.

"I have no way of knowing that, but if they do, I didn't tell them," he said.

"Do you happen to know who runs the club at the moment?" Grace asked.

"I don't have a clue," Donald Rand said.

"I do," I said as it began to sink in.

"Don't keep us in suspense, Suzanne. Who is it?"

"They just held a new election a few weeks ago. Barry Vance is in charge now."

"Barry? But he's moving to Florida," Grace said. "He told us so himself. Why would he kill Gray to get control of his money, just to leave town when he had a chance to get his hands on it all?"

"I don't know," I said. "It doesn't make any sense."

"Regardless, it's out of my hands," Rand said. "Now, if you two will excuse me, I have some books to balance. I'm going to be here all day as it is."

"We're not going anywhere until we confirm your alibi," Grace said. I was glad that she was with me. It had completely slipped my mind.

"Must we really go through this?" he asked.

"We must," I said. "And no coaching her when we get inside. Do you understand?"

He just laughed. "Suzanne, do you think there's any chance I can get Evangeline to do anything that she doesn't want to do?"

"Probably not, but don't even try," I said.

We all walked back in together, and Donald asked her, "Evangeline, could you please tell these ladies what we were doing the night Gray Vincent was murdered?"

She frowned. "Why do they need to know?"

"It will make my life easier if you do. Isn't that enough?" Donald Rand asked.

"Certainly. Very well. We were together in my kitchen

upstairs. I've been working on some of my own homemade confections, and I was trying out new fudge recipes."

"When did you finish up?" I asked her.

"Oh, it must have been well past midnight," she said.

"How did the fudge turn out?" I asked. I had no reason to trust her answers, and I wondered if she'd be able to give me any specific details about her attempts.

"I understirred the first batch, overstirred the second, and with the third, I used entirely too much peanut butter."

"Do you happen to have any I could taste? I just love homemade fudge," I said.

"I haven't thrown any of it out," she said, looking delighted. "Come in back with me."

We all followed her into the backroom, where we found sheets and sheets of fudge waiting for us. I tapped one, and my knuckle sank in. The next was hard as a rock, and the one with too much peanut butter looked as though a single bite would be impossible to swallow. "Take your pick," she said as she offered me a small knife.

I was afraid the overdone fudge might snap off the blade, and the one with too much peanut butter would be so overwhelming I might not be able to choke it down, so I cut a small wedge of the soft fudge and took a bite. Sugar crystals grated on my teeth as I managed to swallow the messy bite. "It's not too bad," I said.

She shook her head. "It's dreadful, and I know it." Evangeline turned to Donald. "You were right. I'm going to throw all of this out and start over."

To my surprise, the financial advisor took her hands into his and said softly, "Don't worry, sweetheart. You'll get it. I have faith in you." Who was this man?

She smiled. "Thank you. Now, if that's all, ladies, this fellow has an arduous task ahead of him."

"Thank you for your time," I said.

"Come back anytime," she said. "I've heard so many good things about your donut shop, Suzanne."

So, she had known who I was, and what I did as a day job. "You should come by. I'll treat you to a donut."

"Thank you, but it's all I can do to resist all of this," she said as she walked us out and gestured to the candy all around her. "I'm afraid your donuts would be my downfall."

I grinned at her. "That's why I've never been in here myself, but now that we've met, I just might make an exception. Just don't let me have anything while I'm here," I said.

"Only if you promise to do the same for me," she answered. "Aren't we a pair?"

"Two birds of a feather," I said.

Once Grace and I were back on the road, I said, "So, we can eliminate Donald Rand."

"Do you believe her?" Grace asked.

"You saw that fudge. I'm willing to bet that she was telling the truth. It's hard to make. Momma can do it, but I've never been able to master the art of it."

"She found a friend in you, didn't she?" Grace asked, laughing.

"We're kind of in the same line of work," I answered. "Neither one of us offers anything that's fit for a steady diet, but they sure do add a little sweetness to life. What's wrong? Do you doubt her story?"

"I wasn't sure until I saw that fudge. I'm sure she didn't whip up three bad batches just to give Donald Rand an alibi."

"So, that leaves us with Gladys and Barry Vance," I said.

"And Barry is less likely now than he was before," Grace added.

"It doesn't make sense that he'd leave town just as he was about to get his hands on half of Gray's fortune."

"If he knew about it," Grace said, "and if he didn't find the other half already."

"Does the mailman seem to you like someone who would be content with half of anything?" I asked her.

"No, it's doubtful, though he might have a hard time stealing money from the garden club."

"I've got a hunch he's resourceful enough to find a way to skim a good bit off the top," I conceded. "It begs the question, though. Did he even know the club was getting half of Gray's money?"

"I'm wondering if Gladys knew she'd been set to get the other half if she'd accepted his proposal? If she thought it was a done deal, she might be tempted to do something before he could change the papers back."

"Only she didn't know that he'd never made it official in the first place," I said.

"I hate that she's back on our radar," Grace said.

"So do I, but we need to know what she knew, what she thought, and get a general timeline of it all."

"How do we find any of that out?"

"There's only one way that I can think of. We have to ask her and hope we can tell whether she's lying to us or not," Grace said.

"Trish is not going to be happy," I said, "but we really have no choice."

"So, it's back to April Springs," Grace answered. "I wonder how Stephen is doing with Mickey Wright?"

"You could always call him and find out," I suggested.

"No, thanks," she replied with a grin. "But feel free to touch base with him yourself if you're that curious."

It was my turn to smile. "I wouldn't have called Jake when he was in charge, so I'm not about to call your boyfriend. We'll find out when we find out."

"Maybe so, but there may be another way we can check things out," she said. "The drive back takes us close enough to Gray's house to make a quick detour."

"Do you think that's wise, especially given the fact that Wright is probably wounded? What if he tries to carjack us and steal your company car?"

"Then we run over him and call it a day," Grace answered with a chuckle.

"Could you really do that?"

"Probably not, unless he was threatening you. Then all bets would be off."

"That's sweet," I said. "I'd run him down for you, too."

"Why wouldn't you? I'm even more fun to be around than you are."

We both laughed, and the rest of the drive was uneventful.

Until we got close to Gray's place and found ourselves facing another roadblock.

This time literally.

CHAPTER 20

"WHAT'S GOING ON?" GRACE ASKED the officer as she rolled to a stop.

"Sorry, but you can't go any farther. There's a turnaround right over there you can use," he said. He was unfamiliar to me, and I noticed that his uniform was from Union Square and not April Springs.

"Is the local chief around?" Grace asked. "I'd like to see him."

"No can do," the officer said.

"Let's just go," I told Grace. "We'll catch up with him later."

"Fine," she said, but it was clear that she was a little miffed about being denied access, whether to her boyfriend or the crime scene, I couldn't say.

Grace turned around, but the moment we were out of sight of the roadblock, she pulled over and grabbed her cellphone.

"Who are you calling?" I asked, as if I didn't already know.

"Stephen," she said.

I didn't even try to stop her. After all, I wanted to know what was going on myself. Would I have called Jake if the circumstances had been different and he'd still been in charge? I was glad that I didn't have to make that decision.

"Hey, it's Grace. I know. I just got stopped by a cop. Okay. Yes. Sure. Fine. Bye." She hung up and then turned to me. "He's busy."

"I'm not surprised," I replied.

"He did have time to tell me that they found blood at the

scene. Mickey Wright was clearly hit by the shot. They followed the trail of blood through the woods, but it dead-ended at the road."

"So, he made it back to his car," I said.

"As a matter of fact, he didn't. They found it half a mile farther down the road, hidden in some trees. He never made it that far."

"So, he carjacked somebody?" I asked.

"They think so, but they aren't taking any chances. They're still scouring the woods in case he doubled back. Stephen said that it wasn't safe for us here."

"He's probably right," I agreed. "Don't worry. They'll catch him."

"I hope so," Grace said as she headed to the diner. "In the meantime, we need to talk to Gladys. I'm not sure who I'd rather face at this moment, Trish or Mickey Wright."

"I'm not, either."

We got to the diner and found Trish Granger frantic, an odd state of mind for her normally. "Suzanne, Grace, when's the last time you two spoke with Gladys?"

"We saw her outside the police station this morning. Trish, I swear, we didn't say anything bad to her."

I was all set to be attacked, but instead, Trish just said, "I'm not accusing either one of you of anything. She never showed up for her shift! Hilda had to stay on, and she's not very happy about it. Me, I'm worried about Gladys's safety. Where could she be?"

"I don't have a clue," I said. "She told the police chief she felt bad about what happened to Gray. She felt responsible, but she didn't say anything about just taking off."

"We need to find her," Trish said. "She might be in trouble. I'm going with you."

Or on the run, I thought, but I kept it to myself. I wondered if that visit to the police station was enough to set her off and send her packing. She'd been distraught. Had she decided to just leave town rather than face what had happened?

"You're needed here," I said as Trish started to leave her diner. "Grace and I will look for her."

"We sure will," Grace agreed.

"I should be out looking for her, too," Trish protested.

"Tell you what. We'll look on our own for an hour. If we don't find her, you can close the diner and come with us. What do you say? That should at least get you through your lunch rush." The place was packed, and I knew if she shuttered her doors now, she'd lose quite a bit of money, and maybe even some longtime customers.

"Okay. I guess that would be all right. Find her."

"We'll do our best," I said. "Where does she live? We'll check her place first."

"I've already called there three times," Trish said.

"Maybe she doesn't want to pick up," I suggested, not wanting to bring up the possibility that she was ignoring her boss while she prepared to leave town.

"Okay. She's at 324 Grosscup, apartment number 6."

I knew the complex. "Got it."

"Call me the second you find anything out," Trish demanded.

"I promise," I said.

Once Grace and I were outside, she looked at me and asked, "Do you think she's on the run?"

"I was just wondering the same thing," I admitted. "She was pretty shaken earlier."

"I think there's a good chance when we get there, all of her stuff will be gone," Grace said. "Trish is going to be heartbroken if Gladys leaves."

"Let's try not to jump to any conclusions," I said.

"What do you know? Her car is still here," I said as we pulled in beside it.

"Maybe she's just not finished packing yet," Grace said.

"If she's planning to skip town, we need to stop her."

"Because of Trish?" Grace asked me.

"That, and because we haven't fully cleared her yet, either. She's still got to be a suspect." I walked up to the door of the apartment and rang the bell.

There was no response.

I rang again as Grace pounded on the door. "Open up, Gladys. We're not leaving until we've talked to you."

More ringing, more knocking, but still no response.

"Do I need to call Chief Grant and get him over here?" I asked. It was an idle threat. The police chief had enough on his hands at the moment, but I was hoping that Gladys wouldn't know that.

"Don't do that," I heard her muffled voice say through the door.

"Let us in," I said.

"I can't."

"Then we're calling Stephen," Grace said.

After a moment's hesitation, I heard Gladys remove the chain, and the door opened, but just a crack. "I can't talk right now. You both need to go." The woman looked terrified to see us. What was going on?

"All we need is two minutes," I said. "You owe us at least that much."

"I can't," she said, her eyes darting behind her. "I'm busy."

Something was definitely going on. "Okay. Sorry to bother you." We needed to get away from that apartment and call the police chief after all. Gladys was in trouble.

Evidently Grace missed Gladys's panic.

Taking out her phone, she said loudly, "You've left us with no choice. I'm calling Stephen."

"No, I don't think you are," Mickey Wright said as he showed himself from behind the door. There was a knife close enough to Gladys's throat to kill her before we could stop him, even if we had a gun, which we didn't. "Come on, ladies. It's time we had a little chat."

CHAPTER 21

WE HAD NO CHOICE.

We did as we were told and stepped inside.

"I'm sorry I got you into this," Gladys said. She was eerily calm, as though she'd accepted the fact that we were all going to die.

I wasn't quite ready to give up yet, though.

Once we were in the apartment and the door was deadbolted again, I could see the massive bandage on Mickey Wright's shoulder. "Are you okay?"

"Spare me your concern," he said, wincing a little as he moved. He clearly wasn't doing very well, but I still wasn't sure we could overpower him without one of us getting hurt, even with his injury. We were going to have to bide our time and wait for the perfect opportunity to strike.

"How did you manage to get here?" I asked him.

"I drove out to Gray's place," Gladys said. "After we spoke with the chief, I needed to be near him. I know it doesn't make any sense, but I felt so bad about what I'd done that I couldn't take it. I was sitting in my car near the entrance to his place when *he* suddenly appeared."

That made Wright chuckle a little, which led to another wince from him. "I couldn't have asked for better timing. As we were driving off, the cops set up a roadblock just behind us."

"What are you going to do with us?" Grace asked, starting to edge away from me. Was she going to make a move now?

We didn't have anything to fight back with, and if we tried something now, I had a sinking feeling in the pit of my stomach that one of us was going to get hurt, or worse.

"Get back over there with your buddy," he said as he lunged a little toward Gladys with the knife. The message was clear. If we tried anything, the cook was going to be the first one to die.

Grace quickly moved beside me again as she mouthed the word, "sorry." I shrugged. We were stuck, and we knew it.

"Grace asked you what your plan was. Do you even have one, or are we going to sit here until someone else wonders what happened to us?"

Wright frowned. "We'll hide here until it's dark, and then you three are going to be my hostages. Now shut up and let me think." He turned to Gladys. "I need some coffee."

"Sorry. All I've got is tea," she said.

He frowned in disgust. "I guess it will do. Go make us some."

As she started to walk away, he said, "Hold on a second. You. Come over here."

He was gesturing to Grace, but I stepped forward instead. If he was going to switch hostages, he was going to use me instead of my best friend.

"Not you. You."

Grace did as she was told, and all I could do was watch. Maybe that was better anyway. Wright only needed one of us to use as leverage in case he got stopped on the road, and Gladys and I would be more trouble than we were worth. No doubt he'd kill us first, but if it meant that Grace had a fighting chance, I was willing to sacrifice both of us for it.

We weren't anywhere near that stage yet.

As Gladys made her way into the kitchen, Wright told her, "If you do anything stupid, both of your friends are dead. Do you understand?"

"I do," she said.

As she busied herself making tea, I asked, "Why did you kill Gray so fast? Clearly you didn't find the money. It seemed kind of hasty to me."

Wright shook his head in disgust. "I didn't kill him! Do you think I'd be that stupid? After I found the cash, maybe, but I was as surprised as anyone else that he was already dead when I got there."

The criminal had no reason to lie to us, and besides, his logic matched ours. Mickey Wright was a lot of things, but he was no fool. "How did you find Gray in the first place? He hid himself so well."

Mickey laughed. "The fool sent me a letter asking me for forgiveness, if you can believe it. He was going to turn himself in after that idiot Bloomfield published his stupid little book about what we'd done. Gary was in love, if you can believe that. With her," he added as he gestured to Gladys in the other room. "Worse yet, he said that he wasn't going to keep any of the money; he was going to give it to charity, some garden club. I wasn't going to let that happen, so I headed straight here."

Gladys must have been listening in from the kitchen. "I can't believe how wrong I was about him. He really did love me, and someone killed him before I could tell him that I loved him, too."

"That money is still out there somewhere," Wright said with resignation in his voice, "but at this point, I'm cutting my losses. Whoever finds it is welcome to it. I just want to get out and never come back."

"The tea's ready," she said.

"Got any sugar?" he asked her as she brought out the tray and set it down.

"It's already been added," she said. One cup's handle was pointed toward Mickey Wright, while the other three were all pointed away. When I caught Gladys's eye, she glanced strongly down for a moment before looking quickly away.

Had she doctored his mug with something? As she reached for a mug to hand to him, Wright said, "Not you. You, donut lady. Give me one of those mugs. She's not going to try to poison us all."

He was being clever, but Gladys might have outsmarted him. I grabbed the mug with its handle pointing toward our captor and handed it to him.

He wouldn't take it, though.

"Take a sip first," he ordered.

"Do you want me to drink your tea?" I asked, wondering just what Gladys had put in it.

"Not all of it, but you need to take a healthy swallow," he said.

I did as I was told, leaving it in my mouth for a moment and then silently letting the liquid back into the cup. Hopefully whatever it was wouldn't hurt me too much, but if it saved the two other women, I would accept that as a worthwhile sacrifice. It was acidic, and I wondered if that was the tea, or what she'd dosed it with.

Wright watched me for a few moments, and then, apparently satisfied that it hadn't been poisoned, he downed his in three quick swallows. "That's some nasty tea, lady. What was it?"

"It's my personal blend," she said. "I know for most folks that it's a little bitter, but that's the way I like it."

"Whatever," he said. "Go on, you might as well serve them, too," Wright ordered me, and I gave each woman a cup, and then I took one for myself. "Now settle in. We're going to be here a while."

After ten minutes of near silence, I saw Wright shake his head, as though he were trying to stay awake. I felt a little sluggish myself, and I hadn't even swallowed any of it, at least not on purpose.

"Move over to the couch." He gestured to Grace and then pointed to Gladys and me. "You two need to sit down on the floor." His words were slurring a little. Had he even noticed? We did as we were told, and it took everything in me not to stare at him as whatever Gladys had used began to take effect. He kept nodding off, fighting it, shaking his head, and then nodding off again.

I heard something hit the floor, and when I looked over, I saw the knife there.

Mickey Wright began to softly snore.

As Grace grabbed the knife, I asked Gladys, "What was in that? Am I going to die?"

"It was just my sleep meds," she said. "You might get a little drowsy, but you should be okay."

"How about him?" I asked.

"He got enough to knock a horse off its feet," she said with a small smile.

"Still, maybe we should tie him up anyway," I suggested.

"There's some rope by the back door. I keep all kinds of things in a bucket out there that I might find a use for later."

"I'd say this qualifies," Grace said as she went to retrieve it.

"That was brilliant," I told Gladys.

"What, dosing his tea?"

"That, and pointing the mug handles the way you did," I said. I was starting to feel bad about thinking Gladys had killed her boyfriend. "I'm sorry about everything."

"I should be apologizing to you. I can't believe I put you both in harm's way."

"What could you do? You tried to warn us, but it took us too long to get it."

"At least it's over now," she said.

"What's keeping Grace?" I asked. "How long does it take to grab some rope?"

"It's not the rope that slowed her down," Barry Vance said as he led Grace back out into the living room. "She ran into a little trouble along the way." He had a gun, and it was pointing straight at my best friend's back.

It seemed that we'd dodged one bad man, but we had one more to deal with before we were home free.

I just hoped we managed to succeed again, though the odds probably weren't in our favor this time.

CHAPTER 22

"YOU READ THE LETTER OF apology Gray wrote to Mickey, didn't you?" I asked him as he led Grace into the room.

"It's amazing what a little steam will do to the glue on the back of an envelope," he said with a twisted grin. "I'm just glad some folks still use the regular old mail to communicate."

"How did you know to check Gray's outgoing mail, or do you snoop around in everyone's business?" Gladys asked him. The fight had gone out of her. She'd bested one foe already, and it appeared that was her limit. Now she was in some kind of stupor, almost like a standing coma. Clearly, it was going to be up to Grace and me to handle this one.

"I've suspected he was up to something for years," he said, "but I was never able to prove anything. I knew he wasn't who he said he was, but that didn't make it easy to figure out what he was really hiding. And then he made a mistake."

"Trying to atone for his past sins," Gladys said.

Barry grinned again. "Kind of bit him in the end, didn't it? I heard a stranger was in town asking around about him, so I knew that I had to act quickly. When I threatened Gray, he offered me a briefcase full of cash if I'd just leave him alone."

"Why didn't you just do as he asked?" Gladys asked, tears streaming down her cheeks.

"You're kidding, right? He would have told the police the second I left," Barry said. "Besides, I couldn't spend the rest of my life looking over my shoulder, waiting for him to track me down. I had to do something, but I had to make it look as though that guy did it, not me," he said as he gestured down at the sleeping Mickey Wright, who had stopped snoring and now looked dead. How much sedative had Gladys used?

"That still doesn't explain what you're doing here," I told him. I wasn't just trying to stall him. I really wanted to know.

"I was on my way out of town when I spotted Gladys driving erratically. As I got a closer look, I saw someone had a knife to her throat from the backseat."

"So you followed her home so you could help her? Forgive me, but you don't strike me as a good-Samaritan type."

"I'm not," Barry said. "I knew who it had to be kidnapping her. If Wright was still alive, the police might figure out that I took the money, but if he were dead, and I planted a bit of the cash on him for good measure, then I'd be home free. I waited outside for him to take care of you three so there would be no witnesses, but you ended up killing him for me. What I didn't know was whether he told you anything or not before you whacked him, and I couldn't take that chance." He nudged Mickey with his foot.

To his surprise, the unconscious man moaned a little.

Barry looked at us, the surprise painted on his face. "You didn't kill him?"

"No, we just knocked him out," I said.

"Then maybe somebody should go ahead and tie him up with that rope. After all, I can't watch all of you."

"Fine," I said. "Give it to me, Grace."

I took the rope from her hands, and I knelt down to tie the thief's wrists together. Where was that knife he'd tried to use against us? I couldn't see it close by, so it wouldn't do me any good. I intentionally botched tying Mickey Wright's hands together and made it clear to Barry as well.

"You have to do better than that," he said. "Do you want him to wake up and cause me trouble? Is that it?"

"I'm sorry. I've never tied anyone up before," I said.

"You do it," he said to Grace. As she knelt beside me, Barry leaned forward to keep a closer eye on us. The gun was still pointing in our general direction, but for a split second, it wasn't aimed directly at any of us.

Grace must have noticed it at the same time that I did. Just as we were about to lunge for the weapon, Gladys surprised us by throwing herself onto Barry's back. We took advantage of his confusion, and we grabbed the gun at the same time, wrestling Barry for possession of it.

It went off in our hands, but fortunately, no one was hit by the stray bullet.

The next instant, the front door imploded, and Chief Grant came barreling through with an entire contingency of cops, both his and some borrowed from surrounding communities.

"How long have you been out there?" I asked him as he took possession of the gun. The men seemed to fight for the privilege of cuffing and dragging both of our would-be assailants out.

"Since Barry pulled the gun," Chief Grant said. "Trish was frantic when she didn't hear from you, so I came over here to see what was going on. We saw Grace's car out front, and Gladys's, too, and when I peeked in through the drapes, I saw Mickey Wright laying on the floor, and Barry holding a weapon on you." He hugged Grace fiercely for a moment and then smiled at Gladys. "We were about to risk a move when you leapt onto his back. That was fast thinking."

"Who was thinking?" the older cook asked. "I didn't want him killing Suzanne and Grace because of me."

"Well, between the three of you, you made sure that wasn't going to happen. Is anybody hurt?"

"No, but I'm still a little woozy," I admitted. "I drank some of the doctored tea."

"Let's get you home," he said.

"I'm all for that," I answered.

CHAPTER 23

TWO DAYS LATER, I WAS running the donut shop with Emma as usual, glad that things were finally back to normal, though Jake was still in Raleigh. It had taken everything I had to tell him not to rush home, and since he was close to dealing with the situation there, he had reluctantly agreed with me. They'd found the missing two hundred thousand dollars in cash at Barry's place stuffed under his lumpy mattress, and the garden club was about to get a double dose of money from Gray's estate. In a way, it was fitting that the landscaper's money would go to a cause dear to his heart.

Just before I was set to close, Emily Hargraves came in, owner of Two Cows And A Moose, and she was beaming. "Have you heard the news?"

"About?" I asked, hoping that nothing else bad had happened.

"Max won the customized quilt!"

"That's great," I said, having nearly forgotten about the charity raffle that had been held as a fundraiser. "What's he getting put on it, famous actors?"

"No, it's even better. Cow, Spots, and Moose are going to be featured, front and center, and when it's finished, it will be displayed proudly at the newsstand. I just hope it doesn't go to their heads." Emily treated her three stuffed animals from childhood as though they were alive, and anyone who wanted to be her friend went along with it.

"What are they going to be wearing?" I asked. Emily was famous for dressing them all up in the most wonderful costumes anyone could imagine.

"I've been giving it some thought, and I think I want them just the way are."

"Are they okay with that?" I asked her with a grin.

"They think it's wonderful," she said as she grabbed a coffee and an overly embellished donut, as was her custom. "Where's Jake? I haven't seen him around lately."

"He's visiting his sister and her kids in Raleigh," I said.

"How long is he going to be gone?"

"Hopefully not too much longer," I said, and then, to my delight, the front door opened again, and the next thing I knew, my husband was wrapping me up in his arms. "You're home!" I shouted.

"Easy, I'm right here," he said as he finally pulled away. "Hi, Emily."

"Hey, Jake. Welcome home. Well, I'd better be going. I just wanted to tell you the good news."

"What's that?" he asked.

"Suzanne will tell you," she said with a grin.

"She won a quilt," I said quickly. "I wasn't expecting you. Did you take care of things with your sister?"

"It's all over," he said. "That guy won't be bothering her anymore."

"Jake, you didn't do something to him, did you?"

"No, not that I wasn't considering it, but he decided to hold up a liquor store, and he got caught doing it. That's why I had trouble finding him. Where he's going, he won't be a problem for Sarah for a very long time." He kissed me soundly, and then he said, "I missed you."

"I missed you, too," I said, happy to have him back where he belonged. "The next time you go anywhere, I'm going with you."

"You've got yourself a deal. How are you doing?"

"Now that you're back? Never better," I said with a huge grin.

"I feel the exact same way."

He stayed with me as I closed the donut shop for the day, and after we went to the bank, we went back home to our cottage together. I knew the Garden Club was going to be feeling rich after their windfall, but they couldn't compare to how I felt.

I had my husband back, a job I loved, and I was surrounded by family and friends.

If that wasn't rich, I wasn't interested in whatever else it might be.

RECIPES

Super Pancakes

My family calls these super because they go well beyond the boxed mix I use as my base. I take any basic mix available off the supermarket shelf, but instead of using it as it is, I like to add leftover goodies I may find in my pantry or refrigerator that might give them a super charge! In the past, I've used things like: diced apples, diced peaches, or diced strawberries; canned pumpkin; raisins; quick oatmeal; or basically anything I have on hand to embellish the recipe to make it more substantial. You can try this with boxed waffle mixes as well. One word of warning. Don't use too much filling so that it overwhelms your basic mix. In addition, I like to add some vanilla extract, cinnamon, nutmeg, allspice, or whatever I'm in the mood for at the moment.

Ingredients (per the mix directions)

- 2 1/2 cups pancake mix
- 2 eggs, beaten
- 1 cup water
- 1/4 cup canola oil

Extras (mix and match)

- 1/2 cup quick oatmeal (uncooked)

- 1/2 cup diced fruit (apple, peach, strawberry)
- 1/4 cup raisins or craisins
- 1 tablespoon vanilla extract
- 1 teaspoon cinnamon
- 1 teaspoon nutmeg
- 1 teaspoon allspice

Directions

Combine the mix's main ingredients as directed. Then choose your extras from the list above, or be creative and try something different yourself. These mixes aren't very expensive, so if something doesn't work, you haven't committed too much to the experiment! I would recommend you add the oatmeal, vanilla extract, and the cinnamon as a base for any recipe. In fact, if that's where you want to start, this alone creates a delicious breakfast all by itself. The diced fruit or pumpkin add heft to the recipe, but you will have to adjust the water you use in the mix. Just try for a consistency of normal pancake mix and you should be fine. This is not an exact science for me, so don't be afraid to play around with it. Once you've got a mix you like, cook the pancakes on the griddle as directed and enjoy.

Makes four to five pancakes, depending on their size

Smashing Good Chocolate Donuts

Every now and then we get on a health kick and forgo our regular fried donuts and make baked ones instead. You didn't think I was going to say that we cut them out altogether, did you? If you did, then you clearly don't know me and my family! These chocolate donuts are delicious, and even friends who swear they don't like baked donuts line up for this one! Imagine a chocolate cake in the form of a donut, and you'll be close to visualizing these. The kitchen smells amazing long after these have finished baking. They can be covered with icing or eaten plain, but my favorite is to sprinkle the tops with powdered sugar. Not only are they delicious, but they are miniature works of art, too!

Ingredients

- 1 cup flour, unbleached all purpose
- 1/2 cup unsweetened cocoa powder
- 1/4 cup semisweet chocolate chips
- 1 1/2 teaspoons baking soda
- 1/4 teaspoon salt
- 3/4 cup milk (whole or 2% are fine for the recipe)
- 1 egg, beaten
- 1/2 cup dark brown sugar
- 3 tablespoons unsalted butter
- 3 teaspoons vanilla extract
- 1 vanilla bean seeds (optional)

Topping

- powdered confectioners' sugar

Directions

Preheat the oven to 375 degrees F.

In a large bowl, mix the flour, cocoa powder, baking soda, and salt together until blended, then add the chocolate chips to the dry ingredients. In another, smaller bowl, combine the milk, egg, brown sugar, melted butter, vanilla extract and vanilla beans (if used) together. Add the wet ingredients into the dry, stirring until they are incorporated together.

Bake 6-9 minutes, or until a toothpick comes out cleanly, then remove the donuts to a cooling rack and dust immediately with powdered confectioners' sugar.

Yields 10–12 donuts.

Fudge Fudge Fudge!

This is a favorite around the winter holidays at my house, but honestly, is there ever a bad time for fudge? Some members of my family love the chocolate (which substitutes a cup of chocolate chips and a cup of chopped nuts for the peanut butter), but this is one of the rare cases where I opt for another flavor instead: peanut butter! There's something about this that takes me back to my childhood, and I love reliving happy memories while I'm creating a tasty treat, too! Be warned, as it happened to Evangeline in the book, making fudge, at least in my experience, is a complex process that's not necessarily easily mastered, but it's worth learning. I've found that the key is the amount of stirring required, as Evangeline discovered herself. Stopping too soon or mixing too long can lead to unhappy results, but the technique can easily be learned, so have patience. Good luck, and enjoy!

Ingredients

- 2 1/4 cups granulated sugar
- 3/4 cup evaporated milk
- 1 cup marshmallow cream
- 1/4 cup unsalted butter
- 1/4 teaspoon salt

Later

- 1 cup peanut butter, smooth
- 1 teaspoon vanilla extract

Directions

In a heavy 2-quart saucepan, add the sugar, evaporated milk, marshmallow cream, butter, and salt. Cook over medium heat, stirring constantly until the mixture comes to a boil. The mixture will be bubbling all across the top, so don't be alarmed, but do be careful, as it's extremely hot at this point! Keep boiling and stirring this mixture for approximately fifteen minutes, and then take it off the heat immediately. With practice, you'll be able to tell when the fudge is finished cooking by its stiffness. Let me warn you, stirring will be a workout near the end, as it becomes quite dense.

Off the heat, stir in the peanut butter until it is thoroughly incorporated, and then add the vanilla extract last.

Quickly spread the mixture onto a buttered 8-inch square pan, let cool, and then cut into small squares.

Makes 36 small squares, a fair amount given the richness of the fudge

If you enjoy Jessica Beck Mysteries and you would like to be notified when the next book is being released, please send your email address to **newreleases@jessicabeckmysteries.net**. Your email address will not be shared, sold, bartered, traded, broadcast, or disclosed in any way. There will be no spam from us, just a friendly reminder when the latest book is being released.

Also, be sure to visit our website at jessicabeckmysteries.net for valuable information about Jessica's books.

OTHER BOOKS BY JESSICA BECK

The Cast Iron Cooking Mysteries
Cast Iron Will
Cast Iron Conviction
Cast Iron Alibi
Cast Iron Motive

Made in the USA
Lexington, KY
14 September 2019